Sweet Temptations: The Boss's Daughter

L.M. Mountford

L.M. Mountford
United Kingdom
Sweet Temptations
The Boss's Daughter

Publisher's Note: This is a work of fiction. Names, characters, places, and incidents are a product of the author's imagination. Locales and public names are sometimes used for atmospheric purposes. Any resemblance to actual people, living or dead, or to businesses, companies, events, institutions, or locales is completely coincidental.

Edited by Readabit: Copy Editing and Proofreading Services Est 2018

L.M. Mountford -- 1st Ed.
ISBN: 978-1-913945-28-2

He thought his temptations were over, but they were only just beginning...

Until last week, Richard Martin was just another middle-aged guy. Married to a wife he loved, father to a son he adored, stuck in a dead-end job, just counting the days go by...

Then everything changed.

He made a mistake.

Now to save his marriage, he's going to have to pay the price.

There's just one problem, Scarlet Holmes.

His Supervisor.

She loves to play games with her staff and now, seeming very aware of his little secret, she wants to play a game.

And she always gets what she wants.

Because she just so happens to be The Boss's Daughter.

The Boss's Daughter is the sinfully tempting and long awaited sequel to L.M. Mountford's debut, Sweet Temptations: The Babysitter. It can be read as a stand alone but it's highly recommend you read Book 1. Full of tension and grippingly intense scenes, this next instalment in the Sweet Temptations Series reminds every one by he has been dubbed The Lord of Lust.

About The Author

L.M. Mountford's goal in life is to be unique, a character who stands out from the crowd that you just can't help remembering with a bemused chuckle.

A born and bred country boy from the southwest of England, he knew from an early age that he wanted to write and spent most of his time writing story ideas or playing Star Wars on his PlayStation.

Not much has changed over the years, though his stories have grown decidedly dirtier, and he swapped the Star Wars for Call of Duty.

Dubbed the Lord of Lust in 2019 and a firm believer that nothing sells like sex and violence, he loves writing about hard and gritty romantic thrillers, loaded with action men, sassy heroines, and a whole lot of dirty, sexy heat.

Sign up for L.M. Mountford's VIP newsletter to details of free books, new releases, discounts, ARC opportunities AND receive a FREE steamy read.

Form available on **LMMountford.com**

Bibliography

For a complete reading list, visit LMMountford.com/bibliography/

Collections
Deliciously Sinful Liaisons
Sweet Temptations Box Set
Romancing the Tropics
Just a Number
The Sweet Temptations Series
The Babysitter
The Boss's Daughter
Just Friends Series
Just Once
Broken Heart Series
Broken
Tropical Cocktail Romance
Tequila Sunset
Beneath the Sheets
Confessions of a Trophy Wife
Forbidden Desire
Rogue Warrior
Rogue
Stand-alone Titles
Uncovered
Serving the Senator
Reckless
Training Tracey

AVAILABLE NOW

FOR A LIMITED TIME ONLY READ FOR FREE

ON KINDLE UNLIMITED

Sweet Temptations

IS ALSO AVAILABLE ON AUDIOBOOK!

Don't Miss Out

Sign up for my newsletter and receive weekly updates on my writing progress, cover reveals, public appearances, reviews, and a FREE eBook.

That's right, a free book every week.

And, sometimes even chances to win advanced copies of my next book before anyone else. So, subscribe to my mailing list today, and keep up will all my new releases and special deals, exclusive to my inner circle.
Subscribe via my website

lmmountford.com

Sweet Temptations:

The Boss's Daughter

L.M. MOUNTFORD

Prologue

His back burned and the spray cut clean to the bone as fat wet snakes slithered down his arms and legs, so cold they burned.

Eyes hooded and vacant, Richard watched the run-off collect around the shower drain, swirling around and around. The blood was almost washed away, leaving only long accusing fingers of dark crimson streaking across the porcelain.

Time had lost all meaning. Seconds and hours bled together until...

"Goddamnit!"

He wanted to scream. To shout. To bellow like a bear in a cage, being dragged through the streets for the amusement of a medieval mob, roaring and bawling in a show of futile outrage at the hard, inescapable reality. Yet the pitiful grunt was all he dared with Alexander in the next room, liable to stir at the smallest sound, and Alice sleeping peacefully just across the hall. So instead, he took it out on the shower wall the way an angry child would beat a pillow.

Red-hot knives stabbed between his knuckles and up his arm in a blast of near-crippling agony as he hit the wall hard enough for bone to crack against the porcelain. Regardless, he ground his knuckles into the tile, relishing the agony it induced, needing it and not knowing what else to do.

Then the moment was gone, and Richard was left shivering in the cold, hot tears stinging his eyes. "Wh-what the fuck have I done?" The question rang hollow, even to his ears.

What had he done? He'd fucked his babysitter, a girl almost young enough to be his daughter. He'd cheated on his wife. And, what was worse, he'd loved every fucking second of it. Then he'd fled.

He could still hear Rebecca crying in her room.

Her sobs had chased him out of the Blaire's flat like a pack of hounds snapping at his heels and it had been all he could do to make it back to the flat without breaking his neck. Alice had already gone to bed when he came bursting through the door. Deep down, a more rational part of him was relieved he didn't have to explain to his instinctively suspicious wife why he was getting in so late, or the fact he smelt like sex and his shirt was misbuttoned, but in that moment, all he could think about was a shower. He'd barely spared a moment to look into their bedroom to check on her before jumping into the bath and cranking the water temperature as low as it would go.

Goddammit! What the fuck had he done! Why had he even gone to fix the computer in the first place? It wasn't a vital job. Rebecca might have been in a state, but it could have waited until morning. So, why the fuck had he gone to the fix the bloody computer, when he'd known, he'd just known it was a bad idea.

Alarm bells had gone off the moment Alice had suggested the girl fancied him. He would have pressed her for more, but then she kissed him, and his world had dissolved to just the feeling of her luscious body pressing into his.

It had been much the same the night they first met, when she'd cornered him in The Burning Book's storeroom. He'd been getting a fresh crate of beer when he'd noticed her leaning against the door. He hadn't noticed her slipping in after him, and the sight of the tiny brunet, all curves and smiles in a black wrap-around dress that could only have been painted on, standing there with her hand on her hip almost had him jumping out of his skin.

Only the Lord alone knew how he managed not to drop the bottles in each hand.

Her smile had only grown more sinful when he'd told her she was in a staff-only area. Then, with a cock of her head and a pouting moan, she'd been on him and he'd promptly forgotten all of his fears of getting caught.

Richard would have stayed. He would have, but then Alice's remarks about Rebecca rung in his ears. Suddenly, he couldn't get the girl out of his head and he'd felt so ashamed that he just needed to get away.

The irony of it all did not escape him.

Self-loathing twisting his guts, he opened and closed his fist, working the feeling back into the stiff digits. They all moved. That was good, nothing broken, but they hurt pretty bad and the throbbing in the knuckles was enough to make him wince with each flex. Then again, that was good too. He deserved the pain.

Christ, I need a drink.

The thought came from out of nowhere but had a restorative effect that had Richard thumbing the shower panel. Pulling the curtain back before the deluge had ceased, he stepped out of the bath, grabbed a towel off the rail and, heedless of the water still running down his legs, made straight for the kitchen.

The oven's display showed it was just after two in the morning.

Out of habit, he made to fill the kettle, but then at the last minute opened the top cabinet. The British Empire might have been built on tea, but this called for something stronger. And he needed to get royally shit faced. Rummaging through the various jars, bottles, and tins, he retrieved the mostly full Bushmills they kept for when Alice's parents came to visit, before grabbing a glass from the draining board.

Pouring himself a measure, Richard threw his head back and downed the whiskey. It burned all the way down, but the liquor brought the warmth back, lessening the sickening knot rooted in his gut, so he savoured it all the same, relishing the hard flavour and distinctive aroma that curled up his nose-

"C-C-Christ," he bit out, coughing so violently each breath rasped like sandpaper, and his hand shook as he filled the glass again. This time making it a double, he stowed the bottle, and its now notably emptied contents, back into the cupboard before exiting the kitchen, drink in hand.

The living room had lost all its warmth as Richard half-sat, half-collapsed onto the sofa. Bathed in the soft light of the standing lamp they kept on a timer to dissuade thieves from getting ambitious, inky blackness pooled along the edges of the walls. Long shadows stretched across the floor like the bars of a cell. His cell.

Wary of another coughing fit that might rouse his wife, he only nursed the drink, sipping the dark amber liquid while staring over the rim of the glass at the dark outside the window.

What have I done?

Hardly a frequent or heavy drinker, the Bushmills made his eyes heavy and his head feel light as the alcohol took effect. The question haunted him, ringing through his ears while flashbacks of the last hour played out before his eyes.

His cock stiffened at the memory of Rebecca standing in the doorway in nothing but that robe. The way her slender curves rigged in his lap. The taste of her on his lips. Her breathy pleading as he tongued her clit. The feeling of her tight little cunt exploding around him...

He hated himself for what he'd done. He'd cheated on Alice, broken his vows to her and risked their marriage. He'd used Rebecca, fucked her like a bitch in heat. Then, worse still, discarded her so callously even though he knew, well suspected, she had feelings for him.

God in fucking hell, he was a beast.

A part of him still couldn't believe it. Here in the safety of his home, on his sofa with a glass of whiskey, the night felt like a bad dream. A God damn fucking nightmare. Only he'd woken to it. The night was like a dream he could only half remember, slipping out of his grasp like pale wisps of morning mist curling around his fingers whenever he tried to focus on one moment. All except for those moments. They were sharp and clear and played before his eyes whenever he'd closed them.

What the fuck was wrong with him? He and Alice were finally getting their lives back to a sense of normality... How was he going to look her in the eye again, knowing that he'd... Christ, what would she say? What would she do? He'd ruined everything. And just when it had all seemed to be going so well. In layman's terms-

"I'm fucked." He toasted the declaration by downing the rest of his Bushmills. "Oh God. *Al*, I'm sor-"

The timer on the lamp's plug clicked over, cutting the power.

Darkness consumed him

Chapter One

There was comfort in sleep. The fool and coward's comfort. The comfort of hiding in the dark and fooling himself it had all been a dream.

Caught between sleeping and waking, Richard stared up at the ceiling. Autumn morning half-light crept through the curtains over the bed, turning their bedroom dark and grey. He didn't hear the cars speeding down Stroud Road, trying to beat the early morning rush hour, or the occasional gurgles coming through the baby monitor. Nor see the furniture taking shape in the gloom. He didn't want to wake up.

He wanted to sleep and dream and pretend. Better that than face reality and the consequences of what he'd done. Having to see his wife every day, holding her in his arms, making love to her, looking into her eyes, seeing the love there, and knowing, just knowing, he'd betrayed her.

Yes, he didn't want to wake, but the warm body wriggling beside him made it inevitable…

He blinked when a hand brushed up his side. Long, delicate fingers, feeling up his ribs and across his stomach. Then there was only softness and warmth. And a faint hint of cinnamon.

A sideways glance showed Alice sleeping next to him on a bed of her mahogany tresses. She must have rolled onto his side sometime in the night and, half covered by the quilt, was curling into him, head resting on his shoulder. She looked so peaceful. Content. Utterly oblivious to everything that had taken place through the night.

Her peace tore at him. Yet he was captivated and watched her sleep regardless, her delicate beauty enrapturing him the way the radiance of the moon enslaves a wolf.

He had to tell her, but how? A part of him wanted to confess now and have done with it. To wait would only make things harder, more complicated.

Excuses flitted through his mind. He was drunk. He'd been desperate. It hadn't meant anything. It was the usual line-up of dirt-bag husband excuses. Though he made sure to steer WELL clear of anything even hinting Alice bore some responsibility. That would not go down well.

Once, he even contemplated suggesting Rebecca had instigated it all. That got chucked out as quickly as it came. No matter what, he needed to keep the girl out of this.

As fond as she was of their babysitter, Richard knew his wife well enough to know she did not share her toys. And if that confrontation with Scarlet last night had just been Alice marking her territory...

Then, he had a pretty good idea of what she would do to him.

That thought made the idea of letting her sleep in a little longer, all the more tempting.

"Alice..." he mumbled. She'd think it odd if he didn't wake her. It would make her suspicious…

Alice mumbled something unintelligible in answer. Still more or less asleep, she shifted closer to nuzzle the hollow of his neck.

Richard stiffened at the contact, a shiver of pleasure rippling up his spine.

Her very closeness was an aphrodisiac. The feeling of her pressed against him, long willowy legs brushing over his calf, full breasts crushed against his side through her cropped sleeping sweater. And her mouth. God, that wicked mouth, brushing so softly over his skin, a mere tease of contact, igniting and sending tingling sensations surging through his skin down to the base of his spine.

Suddenly awake, alert, and very aware of that tale-tell stirring between his legs, Richard blinked, then glanced down to see blue-green eyes looking up at him.

For the longest moment, Alice only watched him, lips pursed and eyes bright with a look that had his cock suddenly harder than steel. Then, slowly, she pivoted, propping her head up enough to rest her chin on his ribs. "When did you get in?"

"Late." The vision of her had the words sticking to the back of his throat. "Did you wait long?"

She moaned a low throaty affirmative, placing a soft kiss just above his nipple while, in a tease of friction, one deliciously long leg slid across to straddle his thigh, making Richard all the more aware of the feeling of her body on his. And the dampness pushing against his leg. She was soaked. The silky heat of her arousal burned through her panties as she stretched out, caging him beneath her, as she walked soft butterfly kisses up his torso.

"I couldn't sleep," Alice purred, her words low and throaty without a trace of sleep. She bit down on his earlobe and tugged, fingers teasing down the flat of his stomach to his boxers. "I just kept thinking about you pushing me up against the fridge, grinding this big, hard cock into my pussy." Long fingers closed around him through the cotton of his underwear, holding, squeezing, then rubbing. "It got me so hot. In the end, I needed Antonio…"

Richard had to bite back a moan. Antonio was Alice's name for the B.O.B her friend Samantha had bought them as a gag gift for their 5-year anniversary. The image of his wife stretched out on their bed, her luscious body arching in throes of pleasure as she worked the toy between her legs, turned his cock to steel within her grasp. Until he recalled just what he had been doing while she had been putting on such an exquisite display and the knot of guilt that lodged inside his gut threatened to chase his erection away.

Alice's mouth claimed his, her tongue sweeping in with lush licks that sent tingles shivering up his spine and brought him back to full mast.

She took his mouth hungrily, her lips moving over his, full and soft and completely at odds with the hot demand that seemed at once to make his head spin while keeping his attention fixed solely on her. And all the while, she was stroking him. Slowly, her tiny hand unable to encompass his girth, but pumping him from root to tip in long, knowing motions, had him instinctively rocking into her, grinding his groin against her palm.

God, how did she always know? Know just how to touch him, how to play his body like a fiddle?

It was maddening. He needed to touch her, but no sooner had his fingers swept through the lush fall of silky locks to tease over her spine than she pulled back.

"I-it got me so horny," she panted, trailing hot little kisses down the line of his jaw. "Knowing you could barge in at any moment and catch me playing with Antonio. I wanted you to watch, to see what you did to me, see how wet I got thinking about your big dick," she spoke slowly, every low throaty syllable an intoxicating seduction. "I was right here, riding my B.O.B, waiting for you to come and see what a naughty wife you have. But you never came. Then I remembered you were up there with Rebecca. Is that why you left me all alone?" Her mouth was everywhere, kissing every bit of skin she could reach as she shuffled slowly back...

Her tongue dragged over his nipple, down the plane of his chest to the elastic of his shorts, only to pull away. "A-Alice…"

His wife rose slowly to sit straight backed between his legs, throwing the covers off, and pushing the lush fall of her hair back behind her ears, the pink of her tongue sliding across those full lips as her eyes found his. Then, "Was she a bad girl for you?"

Oh fuck!

"What?" Ice rushed down his spine and it was all Richard could do to keep the panic from his voice. Fuck, she knew. How could he have been so stupid? Of course, Alice knew. How could she not? Now he was-

"Was she a bad girl?" Alice said again, her voice seeming to grow even more playful as she leaned down to where his erection was visibly straining against the confines of his shorts, the slick tip pushing up from beneath the elastic to leave a slick and shiny trail around his belly button. "Was she still wearing that sexy outfit she had on last night? That cute little pink top and those faded jeans."

Warm air rushed over his crown as those full luscious lips wrapped around him through his underwear and slid up to bite the waistband and tug it back to reveal the fullness of his desire. "Or had she changed into something different, something special, for your eyes only? Stockings? High heels. Maybe a pink babydoll-mmm…" She licked him. The point of her tongue slid slowly up the centre of his column in a long drag from base to tip. "Did you like seeing her like that? Flaunting her body for you in a naughty nighty, her ass and legs on full display, those lush tits peeking out, begging to be sucked. And what about her pussy, that tight, juicy little pussy? Did she taste good?"

Mouth dry and desire shivering through him, Richard couldn't stop the words, "So-so goo-oohh!"

Lips stretched wide and cheeks hollowed, Alice took the head into her mouth and sucked him greedily. She took her time, going neither fast nor slow, but with all the determination of a woman who loved giving head and wasn't afraid to let the world know it.

In a dark corner of his brain, Richard knew he should be disgusted with himself. Alice thought they were playing. To her, this was just a game to spice up the mood. She had no way of knowing he had been balls deep inside their neighbour's daughter last night. And to top it all off, instead of confessing his sin, he was letting her give him one hell of a blow job. But he couldn't resist. It had been so long since he'd felt those luscious lips wrapped around his dick. And her eyes…

Fuck, Alice's eyes were incredible. Deep and stormy, they seemed to shift between grey and blue depending on her mood, and he could stare into them for an eternity and never look away. There were times she had brought him to the brink of cumming with just a look.

It was at once too intense, yet not enough, and Richard had to fist the sheets against the urge to grab, claw, and drive her mouth all the way down on his cock. The lush heat of her mouth glided along his shaft, never taking more than an inch or two in. And so slow. Damnit, how can she be so slow…

"A-Alice…"

She pulled off just as slowly, her eyes burning into his all the way. "Mmm-did you make her your new little cock whore? I bet she was just begging for this big dick." She fluttered her tongue over the slit, making his whole cock tingle and his butt clench. Then she was licking him, that little pink tongue sliding up and down his length. "Did you make her beg for your cock?"

He couldn't think or focus on anything but the feel of her tongue. Then she was taking him back into the delicious heat of her mouth, her head bobbing up and down, the delicious suction of those full lips sliding along his shaft, drawing him deeper. It was too much.

"Yes."

Alice moaned her approval, her eyes bright and burning into his as she pulled off. With one small hand still stroking him, she crawled on all fours up the length of his body, slowly, with her body low and back just that bit arched so he could feel the weight of her breasts dragging up his belly, soft and warm through her thin cotton cardigan, before she reared, like Aphrodite rising from her pool to straddle his waist.

"Oh, you're so bad," she purred, and gave him one final stroke before bringing her fingers up to her mouth and sucked them clean with a low moan. "Mmm... I can taste her on your cock. Did she drop to her knees and suck your big, yummy, married dick first? Or did you just bend her over and fuck her brains out?"

Jesus, her games were going to kill him. "N-neither, I-oh..."

The words trailed away in a low moan as she rolled her hips, sliding his cock along her folds through her soaked panties, showing him how wet she'd gotten. Then, with her right hand, she hooked two fingers beneath the garment and pulled it back, exposing her pussy to his gaze.

"Mmm... yeah baby, what did you do?" Alice purred, taking his cock in her left hand and coating his crown in her cream before pressing it hard against her clit with a slow roll-

She stilled, that sweet little mouth dropping in a voiceless gasp as Richard's hands seized her hips and held her fast as he began working his thick crest into her moist heat. "This."

He'd had enough.

Breath seething, Richard could barely contain himself as he pulled her to him. Even after all their years together, and the birth of their son, she was still so deliciously snug, and he could feel her plush walls stretch as he filled her inch by inch until she'd sheathed to the hilt. The perfect fit for his cock.

"Oh… Oh god! Baby wa-wait…" Alice gasped, her eyes unfocused. Reaching back, she grasped his knees to brace herself. "Not so… you're too… too-oh god!"

Breathless, Richard could only nod, her slight movement altering his angle of penetration. It wasn't much. Just enough to send a rush of sensation up his spine as her slick, velvety walls wrapped around his cock, pulsing and sucking him in as deep as he could go.

The prior night was gone and done. Now it was only them and he bit, chewed, and clawed against the instinctive urge to throw his wife on the bed and just take her. It had been weeks since the last time they'd gone a few rounds. She'd need time, time to adjust, time to get used to the feeling of being filled with him. So instead Richard just watched her, drinking in the sight of Alice straddling him, her head tipped back, the bounty of lush mahogany tresses cascading down to the small of her back, the plunging neckline of her cardigan revealing a feast of golden skin as her breasts strained against the cotton, imprisoned from his view by a few struggling buttons.

He wanted to see more. He wanted to see her.

"Mmm… you feel amazing, so tight," he purred, reaching up to tug the button from its fastening, bearing her full and luscious cleavage. "And such beautiful tits."

"Yeah, better than hers?" Alice panted, her back curling in offering as he sat up and took the peak of a single dusky nipple into his mouth.

"Much."

He teased her mercilessly, raining soft kisses down across her breasts, his wily tongue lashing down and around, refusing to pay her nipple any attention. Her skin was growing hot and he could feel her shake in his arms, pleading for more. Yet she held on until he sucked the stiff peak into his mouth, his hands crushing her to him and grinding her down on his cock with just the right amount of force to make her creamy walls pulse around him.

"Liar."

Low and breathy, the heat in her words sent a shiver straight down his spine, moments before long fingers fisted in hair and dragged his head back. Dark and lustful, Alice's eyes burned hungrily into his as she lowered her full lips to his, her lush tongue claiming him in a possessive dance that both thrilled and terrified him. This wasn't part of her game. She wanted him to know he was hers. Her husband. Her lover. He was her man, no matter what, and he'd better not forget it.

She rolled her hips, breaking the kiss and rising until only half of him remained inside her.

"Mmm… Mr Martin," a soft, girlish voice purred. His heart leaping into his throat, Richard's eyes shot up to meet Rebecca's big doe eyes, his wife's sharp, angular face now soft and long. Then, she dropped back down, her lush heat clenching down, like a second mouth sucking him in…

Bolting upright, Richard just managed to brace himself on the armrests of his chair as it righted itself and almost pitched him headfirst into his desk. What the-

Reality caught up with him. He wasn't at home. He was at work in his office.

Sweating, heart pounding and his cock straining against his trousers, he collapsed back into the treacherous piece of furniture. Cupping his hands over his head and dragging his fingers down his face, he did his best to bite down on a sarcastic laugh. "Thank God. Just a dream-"

"Yo Dick, you feeling alright mate?"

Chapter Two

It never ceased to amaze Richard how, even when dressed to meet Holmes & Raine's business dress code, Mark McClaine always had the look of a second-hand car salesman. It was his perpetual grin. With that boot polish-black hair and moustache, it made him look like John Challis's Boycie in Only Fools and Horses, just without the sincerity.

Perched in the open door with his arms crossed, he was grinning at Richard like the cat that had got the cream. "Not looking too good there, Dick. Everything okay at home?"

"Yeah, I'm fine mate." Richard forced a smile. "Just, just got a lot on my mind, that's all."

Mark gave a dry laugh. Then, still grinning, he straightened and strolled over to his desk, the closest to the door, and dropped into his chair. He spun it around to face Richard in the adjoining cubicle. "I bet you do."

Richard did his best to ignore him. Him, and the chill that shivered down his spine. It wouldn't do any good.

McClaine was like a Jack Russell with an old sock whenever he got the sense he was getting under someone's skin. And that was all he had, a scent, an inkling. Just a hunch. He didn't, couldn't know.

He was waiting for him to bite. Richard could see the mirth dancing in his eyes and knew it would be a mistake. So instead, he turned back to his computer. The screen was asleep, but a quick nudge of the mouse brought it alive. Prompted by a security box, he entered his password then watched the various excel spreadsheets pop back up. He bit back a groan. Would it have been too much to ask for a computer virus, or maybe just a good old power cut?

The Prometheus Account.

It had been due well over a week ago, and Scarlet had been on at him to get it done and on her desk by the end of the day.

He'd been working on it all morning, but with everything that had happened, his head just wasn't in the right place. And all the while, Mark had watched him, grinning that inane, shit-eating grin. Just the prospect of a long afternoon of it all over again had him blindly reaching out for his mug of tea. It was cold as ice, but he didn't care.

McClaine cocked a brow. "Ya know that tea's been sitting there all morning, right?"

"Mhm…" Richard murmured, chugging it down, not even tasting it as the memory of Rebecca purring his name in that hot wanton tone burned his ears.

Mr Martin…

"I flushed my pen out in it while you were in the land of nod."

"Mhh-" Eyes widening as the words and the acrid ink flavour registered, Richard pivoted and retched, spitting out the vile mixture into the waste bin beside the desk. "You… asshole!" Coughing, it took everything he had not to hurl the mug at McClaine. What little of his curse made it through the spluttering, however, was lost in the other man's laughing.

"Hey! Why aren't the pair of you out for lunch? Trying to bugger each other over the desk or something?"

Wiping his mouth with the back of his hand, Richard shot a withering sideways glance at Dave Sing. "Or something."

A third generation English-Nepalese, from the generation who had turned their back on the ancestral beliefs and completely assimilated to western culture, Dave Sing was also tall and thin. Handsome, with almond skin and copper eyes, but jet black that hair that he kept short and spiked. He'd joined the firm shortly after Richard, a fresh-faced graduate from Coventry University. Young and ambitious- Richard liked him well enough. An asset to the team, but in dire need of seasoning.

His own lunch in hand, the office's third resident settled in his own seat and was about to take a bite of a generous beef burger when he got his first close-up look at Richard. The burger dropped into its wrapper. "Geez Rich, you look awful."

"Yeah-"

"Yeah, well, what do you expect?" McClaine cut in, just managing to get control of his guffaw. "Ben Dover here had a wild weekend after the do last week."

"What?" Richard rounded on him, his heart in his throat. No, he couldn't know about Rebecca. There was no way he could know, unless-

"Oh, come on, Dick, don't give us any of that old pony. That look your missus got when she saw old Walrus Face's daughter putting the moves on you. You can't honestly expect us to believe you didn't get a little bit. Alice damn near started fucking you right there in front of everyone."

"Fuck off," Richard warned, but inside he felt the knot his insides had wound loosen. Slightly.

McClaine shot Sing a sly look and added under his breath, as if to keep the man sitting just meters away from hearing, "Pity she didn't. What I wouldn't do to see that fine ass bouncing-"

"*Mike!* I'm warning you," Richard growled. "Shut your fucking hole or the next thing out of your mouth will be your teeth." He emphasised the threat by pushing back from the desk and rising to his feet, the rancour contorting his features into a look of such maleficence it had both Sing and McClaine backing away.

McClaine raised both hands in supplication, his face turning pale. "Woah, Dick, woah. I'm just busting your balls. Okay. Okay? I-I I'm sorry. Jeez… just relax. Relax." He was on his feet and backed round the desk.

Richard watched him go, letting him put a bit more space between them before dropping back into his chair.

All the tension seeming to evaporate from the room at once, and McClaine let go of a deep sigh. "We cool? God, my heart's beating so fast I think you were about to give me a coronary."

"Well, you do deserve it from time to time." Richard kept the bitterness from his tone. McClaine was the sort who needed a slap now and then, and he'd enjoyed the opportunity. No matter what, he loved his wife too much to let that sort of slander pass unchastised, but it wasn't worth settling at work. She'd be the first to tell him that. A man has to do what a man has to do, and the first thing a man had to do was to care for his family. Everything else, including giving mouthy gits a smack in the gob, came later.

"Ouch! That hurt. No, seriously mate, what's with you today? You've been bumbling around her like a zombie high off its head."

"Well, can you blame him?" Sing looked up, his burger already much reduced. "You said it yourself. Scarlet has it pretty wet for him. And you've heard the stories."

"Yeah, but come on, you don't believe all that shit, do you? What would she have to gain?"

"What do you mean, what would she have to gain?" Sing looked incredulous; his speech momentarily dissolved into the singsong accent of the Hindu.

"Why would Scarlet want to sleep with Tommy Cox or that asshole Mike in legal? She's a bird. They don't spread their legs for their underlings. What could they do for her? I mean, she's the big boss's daughter. Why should she shag anyone in the firm? If she wants a promotion, or a pony, all she has to do is ask 'Daddy', and Walrus Face will give his little princess anything she wants."

"Please, that is such misogynistic bullshit. A woman can be every bit as abusive as a man. Haven't you read Disclosure?"

"I saw the film," McClaine cut in, and then his features twisted with a leer. "And I tell you, that Demi Moore can suck my cock any day…"

Richard was only half listening to them. He had heard the stories, too. And like McClaine, usually dismissed them as idle office gossip.

Whatever else she might be, Scarlet was undoubtedly a very beautiful woman, and beautiful women in positions of power and authority attracted rumours the way a dog drew fleas. Often as not, they were just stories spread by jealous colleagues or bitter subordinates left in her wake- and Scarlet wasn't short of those. Quite the reverse in fact, but she was also the daughter of the firm's MD, Derick Holmes. The consequence for any employee caught besmirching her good name would be unpleasant, but after their encounter on Friday, Richard was no longer entirely convinced all the stories were *just* stories, but he wasn't about to admit it.

There'd been a look in her eyes. A certain, predatory gleam…

"Okay, that's enough," Richard snapped. "Have either of you actually spoken to anyone who actually fucked her? Or heard a story that wasn't from a guy who spoke to a guy?"

McClaine's grin dropped. "No."

"Well no," Sing admitted, shoving the empty burger box into a desk drawer. "But Jasper Hawkins told me he once saw her going down on the girl from the mailroom." He looked vindicated.

Until McClaine asked, "Umm, Davey-boy, remind me, what happened to Jasper Hawkins?"

Sing shrugged. "Walrus Face kicked him to the curb."

"For?"

"Improper conduct."

Rich barked a triumphant laugh. "Ha! Exactly, telling tales about his daughter. See, he was talking out of his arse and got canned for it. So, with that cleared up, can we get off this subject? I don't fancy getting sued for libel."

"Slander," Sing corrected.

"What?"

"Libel's written. You mean you don't fancy getting sued for slander."

Richard gave him the finger. "Oh, shut it Apu. I don't give a damn. If you have to be so pedantic, why don't you take a look at this," he scouted back, making room for the pair. Sing and McClaine exchanged a look, then pushed back from their own desks and walked around to his. "I told Scarlet I'd get this report over to her this morning, but the numbers don't add up. I don't know. Is there something I'm not seeing?"

"So?" McClaine asked, coming up to peer over Richard's shoulder. "You know the drill. If it doesn't add up, just attach an advisory."

Sing nodded in agreement. "That's company policy."

Hemmed in by the tight confines of the one-person cubicle, Richard felt the room growing noticeably stuffier. "I know, but something just doesn't feel right."

"Geez, Dick!" McClaine exclaimed, slapping a hand down on the desk. "Why are you making this so hard for yourself? You know the bitch has a major stick up her ass about this sort of thing. Just give her the report. It's not your job anymore-"

"Mr Martin?"

The semi that had been slowly diminishing surged to renewed life as Richard's heart leapt into his throat, his head snapping up. And then he was back there in that bedroom, naked, with *her* stretched out beneath him, his cock buried to the root in her lush, grasping heat. That sweet voice hot and panting in his ear.

"Ah... ahhh-oh my God-oh my God-oh my God... I can't take it... it's too much... too big!" she shrieked, her fingers clawing at the walls and eyes wide with pure ecstasy. "Oh yes... yes... don't stop... I'm all yours Mr Martin... I've wanted your hard cock inside me for so long... you can fuck me whenever you want to... just don't stop... don't stop!"

Rebecca stood in the office doorway.

It was the first he'd seen of the girl since their tryst Friday night, and she looked amazing.

Her white button up blouse was smart and conservative, and while too short to reach her knees, that skirt would have to go a hell of a lot higher to offend any granny's delicate sense of decency, or workplace dress code. Yes, there was nothing overtly sexual in her attire, but the thought of what she hid underneath- those lush full tits, her tight athletic build, made it all sexy as hell. And she was gorgeous, too. Her dark chestnut hair had been tied into its customary side braid and there was a little dusting of blusher to her checks, but it was her lips that caught his eyes first. There was a glossiness to them that immediately made him ache to kiss her, taste her…

She must have come straight from work; it was the only time she wore make-up.

"Hi Rebecca." The words sounded feeble, but it was the best he could do on the spot. Though he'd known this moment would eventually come, he'd been so obsessed with what he'd tell Alice, he'd never actually thought about what to say to Rebecca. "What are you doing here?"

"Mrs Martin called. She thought you might be getting hungry." She beamed a sweet girlish smile and held up a plastic bag. "You forgot your lunch."

"Ah… Thanks… Rebecca," he nodded, feeling suddenly embarrassed. He'd been in such a fluster that morning he'd left his Tesco's pasta salad in the fridge and hadn't noticed until he'd been halfway to work. "Just plonk it down over on that cabinet other there. I'll get to it in a bit. How much do I owe you?"

She beamed, sweeping past him and around the desks. "Don't sweat it, it's on me."

"Really?" He pivoted in his chair to follow her. "You sure about that?"

"Yeah, it's nothing. I wanted to check out the Victorian Market anyway, so it's no big deal." Her smile seemed to broaden. "And I got a *big* bonus over the weekend."

A big bonus? Fuck, what did she mean? Richard felt cold fingers trail down his spine. Was she planning to blackmail him, to keep what happened a secret? He wouldn't have thought so. The girl generally had all the sly cunning of a Care Bear. Then again, she had told Alice, and who had secretly told him, that she'd been saving to move out and get away from her father.

Hush-money could go a long way there.

Or was she after something else?

Something more *physical*.

The prospect made the knot in Richard's gut tighten and he was torn between terror and being a little turned on. "That's cool. Well, thanks Rebecca. I owe you-"

"Urh, Mr Martin, could I have a word with you? Um…"

"Ah, well, now isn't really the best time. You caught us at a bit of a bad moment and-"

"Aw, don't be silly Dick, we can spare the girl a moment," McClaine's eyes glittered darkly as he gave the girl a slow, less than subtle once over.

Rebecca quickly twisted away from his scrutiny. "Er-no! No, I understand." Then she gave Richard a sideways glance, a small smile curling those lush pink lips. "If you want, you could just pop round later… If you have the time that-that is, that is, please, I don't want to put you out and my dad will be out so -"

"Ah… No, that's alright." Remembering her standing at the door in that little black *thing*, Richard swallowed. He couldn't be alone with her, not there. He was safe here. This was his work; she wouldn't try anything here.

And more importantly, nor would he.

He glanced nervously at his co-workers. They were both grinning like a pair of mangy hyenas. "Mind giving us a minute, lads?"

"Sure." McClaine gave Sing a nudge. "Come on Apu, let us leave Dick Hefner here to tend to his little lady friend." However, he paused by the door after the smaller man had gone through and threw a sideways glance back at Richard. "Oh, and enjoy yourself Dick, you're more in need of a blow job than any other white man in history."

Bastard.

Richard cursed and turned away, flipping him the V-Sign over his shoulder. It was an almost impotent retort, but it was the best he could do with Rebecca in such close proximity. He couldn't risk over reacting. He couldn't take the chance of giving his work mate cause to think something was going on.

So he kept his attention locked on his screen, even after the door shut and the laughter drowned out by the hum of computer drives. Yet his eyes had a mind of their own and every few moments he caught himself glancing over in her direction as Rebecca jumped up to perch her ripe little derriere on the edge of his desk, her pencil skirt riding up as she crossed her legs to flash him a hint of thigh.

Thighs that had been wrapped around him just days ago.

Growing ever more aware of the stiffness between his legs, while his guts twisted into knots, Richard swivelled around to face her, blindly tapping a few keys to minimise the spreadsheets. Not that he thought she would have any interest in them, but PPI was such a hot topic, better safe than sorry.

Forcing down a dry swallow, he smiled pleasantly at her. "So, what's so urgent?"

"Well… I wanted to… um it's just that… Well…" She looked away, a blush staining her cheeks a dusty pink. "I'm sorry. About what happened on Friday, I don't know what got into me…"

"I think I have some idea." He couldn't help a dry chuckle.

"I didn't mean like that," Rebecca laughed, the sound high and girlish, breaking the tension that had been building between them.

For a moment.

Then the dam broke, and she started to cry. Fat, glassy tears rolled down her checks in rivers. "I'm so sorry, Mr Martin. I didn't mean for it to happen. Please, please don't hate me. I- I couldn't…"

Her tears raked him. "Hey, hey, hey, come here." Richard opened his arms. She all but threw herself at him, burying her face into his neck and sobbing loudly as he hugged her back. "It's okay, sweetheart. It wasn't your fault. Everything just happened so fast..."

Not sure what else to do, he held her till the tears passed, and then he continued to hold her, rocking gently from side to side. It felt good to hold her like this. She felt good. Her hair was silky soft against his cheek. That lean athlete's build fitting against him so perfectly, warm and so very inviting. Those lush young breasts pushing against his chest through the material of her uniform, tipped by dusky nipples that just begged to be sucked.

"Mr Martin?" Rebecca voiced, her tone shaky and uncertain, and he was suddenly aware she was looking down. Down at where the bulge was pitching a tent in his trousers.

Oh shit…

Heat burned across his cheeks as her head tilted back up to his, those full lips curling into a sly feline smirk.

"H-how was the market?"

No sooner had the words left his mouth, he knew they were a mistake.

Only, he had no idea what else to say. The question was the first thing that came to mind that didn't also involve the words fuck, cunt, cock, tits or cum- in one insidious combination or another.

"Oh… It's amazing!" She positively beamed at the question, her big doe eyes lighting up with mischief. "There are so many stalls this year, and the costumes. It's just like something out of Dickens' times."

"That's… nice. Err Rebecca I have to-"

She carried on regardless. "They've even set up a snow machine over the ice rink…"

"Rebecca-"

"But it's broken and…"

"Rebecca… look… I… I don't think-"

"You should hurry up and eat your sandwich, Mr Martin, before it gets cold."

"Rebecca…" He really needed her to stop talking.

"Mmm… it's pulled pork. I had the hog roast sausage. I normally prefer chicken, but when I saw them on the spit, I couldn't resist. They were just so big and thick; I wasn't even sure I could get it in my mouth-"

He took her mouth, kissing her hard and hungrily, drinking in her lushness.

It was madness. Utter madness. But Richard couldn't take it. He had to have her again. Pulling her into his lap, his hands slid down the lines of her narrow waist to cup and squeeze her butt through her skirt, crushing her to him, making her moan and arch. Fuck, she tasted even better than he remembered. There was no trace of cherries now. Only the lushness of her soft pink lips, and she was all the sweeter for it.

Rebecca didn't waste a moment. Burying her hands in his hair, she sucked his tongue like a woman possessed and moaned a low purr that vibrated through him and made his trapped cock throb against its confines.

Yet it wasn't enough. Nowhere near enough. He wanted more. He wanted her, wanted to rip her shirt open and taste those plump tits. Wanted to bury his face between her legs and eat her hot, wet cunt. Wanted to bend her over his desk, go balls deep in that tempting little pussy and fuck her like the hot little bitch she was.

She moaned a pitiful protest when he left her mouth, but it quickly turned to small kittenish gasps as he nipped a fiery trail down the long slope of her neck. Then she was like putty in his hands. Her hands dropped down to push his jacket halfway down his arms, before working on his shirt buttons, fumbling a bit as he sucked the sweet spot where her neck and shoulder met.

"Oh... Mr Martin!" Rebecca moaned, her head rolling back, exposing more skin for him to kiss. He greedily obliged, dragging the flat of his tongue along the dips and hollows of her throat. Meanwhile, his hands ground her on the ridge of his cock, sliding under the hem of her skirt and up to the warmth beneath. Up along the smooth, silky-soft skin of her inner thigh. Fingers stretching, brushing over taught tendons and reaching for the heat of her lush wet-

A door slammed shut somewhere down the hall, and Richard's heart leaped into his throat. He froze, a moment of clarity rushing over him in an icy cascade.

Shit!

"Stop. Stop- shh!" Seizing Rebecca's arms, he pushed her away, quite literally holding her at an arm's length as he threw a sideways look towards the door.

It was still shut, but the window would have given anyone passing by a front-row seat of their own dirty little peep show.

He watched it, not daring to blink.

Ten seconds.

Thirty seconds.

One minute and still nothing.

He let out a breath. That was close. He didn't want to think what might have happened if someone had seen them. Even now, with their flushed faces and dishevelled condition, it wouldn't have taken Doctor-bleeding-Spock to work out what had been going on.

"Mr Martin?"

Rebecca's voice was so quiet and unsure, it was almost a stranger's voice. He twisted back to face her, and the look in her eyes raked his soul. She couldn't have looked more hurt if he had slapped her.

"Rebecca..." The words caught in his throat. He'd seriously fucked up. Again. "We can't do this."

"Why not?"

Richard felt like the lowest piece of shit that had ever walked the earth. "You know why. I'm married, and I love my wife."

"She doesn't have to know."

"That's not the point. Alice deserves better than that, and so do you." Unable to look her in the eyes, he shrugged his jacket back into place before fixing his buttons. "I don't want to use you like that, Rebecca."

"I don't care. You can use me however you want. I-"

The sudden shrill shriek of a phone ringing cut her off. His computer monitor burst into life, and Alice's face stared back at them.

Chapter Three

"Get down," Richard snapped, not exactly pushing the girl away but urging her off of his lap and down under the desk with an insistence that brokered no argument from her. Then, heart pounding like a drum in his chest, he turned back to the screen.

The Skype video call was getting close to timing out.

Resisting the urge to glance down to the girl's hideaway, he accepted the video call, then forced a broad smile. "Hey Al."

His wife's avatar minimised, and Alice's smoky gaze met his.

"Not interrupting anything, am I, *Dick?*" Even wrapped around an insinuation, her husky tone made his dick hard all over again.

Or maybe it was just the sight of her all dressed up in her *'work wear'*. No doubt, the sight of Alice in that tan blazer, button up blouse, and white pencil skirt had fuelled more than a few teenage boys to lock themselves in the toilets for an extended break.

"Nah, just taking my break. How's work?"

"Boring," she pouted. "I seem to spend all day either marking half-term homework or giving out detentions… Errr, I hate November."

"Aww… don't worry, love, it'll soon be Christmas."

She rolled her eyes. "Ha… ha… ha… Don't remind me."

Alice loved her work. She loved being a teacher, but there were times when the job didn't love her. "Speaking of Christmas, you left your lunch at home, so I gave Rebecca a call and asked her to pop in with something special for you."

Her tone was playful, but the edge to her voice sent a shiver down his spine, and he found himself glancing down at the dark space under his desk.

"Yeah… she just left." He picked up his still wrapped sandwich and held it up for her to see.

A ghost of a smile curved the corner of her mouth and the tip of her tongue darted out across her plump upper lip. "Mmm… good, because I have a little surprise for you."

Momentarily lost in all the memories of just what that tongue and mouth could do, Richard could only swallow. "Oh…"

She leaned back in her big black chair and began working on the buttons of her blouse. "I admit I was rather miffed with you over the weekend for getting in so late the other night, but I think I know a way for you to make it up to me…"

Richard couldn't believe his eyes. "Jesus, Alice… are you mad?"

"Come on *Dick*, I don't have long till my next class… mmm… one of my students might come by at any minute…" As the last button came undone, the blouse fell open to tease him with a glimpse of her breasts, full and firm and absolutely luscious, before she pressed it closed.

"Whoopsie…"

"Tease."

"Aww… remember how we used to do this whenever one of us was working late… come on baby…" She let one corner of the garment slide down to reveal her left breast before cupping it. "Mmm… you like these baby, God I wish you were here… I'm so horny… I just want to jerk your big dick off with my tits and watch you paint them with all your yummy cum…"

Richard had to force himself to breathe as he watched his wife raise her tit up to her mouth and swirl her tongue around the pebbled nipple. She knew how much he loved her tits. Knew just how to use them to drive him wild.

"A-Alice…"

"Do you want me to beg for it… want me to get down on my hands and knees… and beg to see your cock…" The blouse fell open completely as Alice pushed her breasts together, making them bounce and jiggle before rolling the dusky nipples between her fingers and thumbs. "Mmm… you're so bad. Do it, Dick, I want your cock."

And his cock definitely wanted her.

That throaty husk of hers had him as hard as steel.

Sensation rippled up and down his length as it fought to be free of its restraints. So insistent and demanding, his white knuckled grip on the armrests of his chair was all that kept him from ripping open his chinos and giving her the show she craved.

Then he felt something brush against his leg.

He froze.

He knew he shouldn't look, but his eyes had a will of their own. Drawn down like magnets to watch the slow seduction of a hand rising from under the desk. Slowly, step by step, walking up his leg bit by bit towards the bulge of his cock, getting closer and closer and…

"Fuck..." A ragged breath left him in a rush as soft digits curled around his imprisoned length and gave it a testing squeeze.

"That's it, grab it baby, tell me how big it is... so big and hard and full of cum..." Alice panted in her hot breathy tone, the fingers of her left hand roughly attending to her nipple, twisting and tugging in the way that always got her hot. "Just thinking about you sitting there, jerking your big dick for me... mmm... gets me so wet. Does it feel good, Dick?"

"Yeah... so fucking good..." Richard groaned, Rebecca's small hand fisting him through his trousers, pumping along his length from root to head, her movements slow but urgent. He tried to focus on the screen, on his wife, to blot out the sensations Rebecca was sending sizzling through him, but he was too finitely aware of her. Aware of her shuffling closer, her head of dark chocolate hair creeping out from beneath the table, her free hand creeping up his other leg. Moving higher and higher towards his zipper.

He needed to stop this. He needed to stop her, but when he tried, his body had a will of its own. Instead of pushing her away, his hands just undid the fastenings of his belt and trousers. Then Rebecca's hand was dragging him from the confines of his boxers, and it was too late.

"Suck it." The command was out before he knew what he was saying.

"Fuck yes, baby, I love sucking your cock..." Alice moaned on the screen, thinking the command was for her. "I really wish you were here. Your cock's so big and tasty. I could suck it all day, jerking you off with my tits until you paint my face with your cum. Or would you just bend me over and pound-pound me... pound me from behind..."

She was getting close; he could hear it in her voice. Richard could imagine her hand under the desk, fingers pushing under the silk of her panties to rub her clit. "Stick it in me Dick. I need it. I've been such a naughty schoolgirl, bend me over your desk and punish me... punish me with it... spank my ass with your cock and use my naughty little pussy... she's so nice and hot and wet for you... just begging to get your dick off- oh shit!"

Through the speakers, the school bell sounded faint and distant, but it hit Alice like ice.

In a flash, she was up and pulling herself together as the hall outside filled with the shouts and bangs of children running to their next class. "Sorry babe, gotta go, but we'll finish this later," she promised, before killing the Skype connection with a click of her mouse.

Richard hardly noticed.

Instead, his eyes never strayed from the vision of Rebecca's big doe eyes staring up at him from beneath her bangs as her pink lips wrapped around his cock. A picture of innocence and wickedness. Then she was taking him in. Those lush lips brushing over his glands and down his shaft. The wet heat of her mouth enveloped him, sucking him in all the way to the gate of her throat, before pulling back to mouth his sensitive crown.

"You've no idea how long I've wanted to do this, Mr Martin," she purred, teasing his underside with slow licks. "I'm sorry, I know it's wrong, but after Friday night, I just can't help myself..."

"It's okay Rebecca, that wasn't... it-it's not your fault."

Richard groaned, his head rolling back as the hand still holding him began pumping up and down.

"It's alright, Mr Martin. I know you're only saying that. It's all my fault. I'm such a naughty girl, going down on you while you're talking to your wife. Have I been bad, Mr Martin?"

"Yeah, so very bad."

"Do you like it Mr Martin?

"*Yes.*" The feeling was so intense that Richard's death grip almost snapped the arms clean off his chair.

"Are you going to punish me?"

"Oh yes, I'm going to put you over my knee alright, and if you don't make me cum quickly, I'll bend you over and fuck you across this desk until you can't walk straight."

"Oh, promises, promises…"

She took him back into her mouth. Her cheeks hollowed as she sucked hard, head bobbing up and down while fisting his root, making up whatever she lacked in experience with enthusiasm.

"Mmm… yes, yes, yes… just like that…" Richard groaned, almost as much for her benefit as for his, the words just tumbling out as he melted back into his chair. His hands lost themselves in the silky softness of her hair. He gathered up and pushed back a wing of dark chocolate that had fallen out of place, before fisting it as the flat of her tongue swirled around his crest once, twice, thri- *oh fuck!*

The sensation came upon him so quickly, he didn't have a chance to voice a warning before his hot cum fired into her greedy mouth. His orgasm ripped through him hard enough for black spots to dance before his eyes, but Rebecca accepted everything he had to give her.

She drank every drop. Swallowing greedily as it flowed, sucking when the tide ebbed. And all the while watching him, those big doe eyes bright with… what?

Satisfaction at having brought him to orgasm so easily?

Or excitement about future possibilities?

Only when she had finally milked him dry and his fingers slipped from her hair did she release his still firm erection and stand back up. Taking the napkin from her uneaten sandwich, she wiped her lovely rosy lips clean. Stepping around his chair, she lent down and pressed a soft kiss to his cheek.

"I better get back. See you later, Mr Martin."

"Rebecca wait-" Richard started, but her cute little derriere was already sashaying out the office, the door slamming shut behind her.

His fist hit the desk, hard enough to make the structure tremble. "Shit!"

You stupid bloody bastard, he cursed inwardly as guilt and shame raked him with claws of ice and fire, respawning the sicking knot deep in his guts. How the fuck could he have been so stupid to of let that happen, again?

A ping sounded from the computer, making Richard's heart leap into his throat. His head snapped up to see the icon for the unfinished report flash. The ping was a pre-programed reminder to warn the user whenever a file had been open and inactive for too long.

Richard contemplated it for a second. "Fuck it!"

Tapping a few keys, he deleted his notes, closed the document and forwarded it in an email to Scarlet's inbox.

They were right. It wasn't his job anymore. What the fuck did it matter, anyway?

Shoving himself into his trousers and refastening his belt, he grabbed his untouched sandwich and took a bite.

Only, he'd lost his appetite.

Chapter Four

"We're heading off, Dick. Catch you later."

Richard looked up from his monitor just in time to glimpse McClaine and Sing trot out the office with backhanded waves, like schoolboys ditching detention. "You guys off already?"

"*Already?* Do me a favour, Dick, take a day off, will ya."

"Go see the girls at Spearmint Rhino. They do your sort of favours, mate, not me."

McClaine shot him a look that could curdle custard, then raised his hand, pulled back his cuff and pointed to his TAG Heuer watch face. "See this? It's past five. That's clocking off time in my book. You might be prepared to work yourself ragged, but I've got better things to do than kill myself for old Walrus Face and little miss Tight Ass. Some of us have a life, ya know, see ya."

"You live with your mother!" Resisting the urge to flip him the finger, Richard turned back to his desk, his eyes landing on a mountain of paperwork. Work he'd been putting off while obsessing over the Prometheus Account.

He checked his own wristwatch, a Seiko his old man had given him for his eighteenth birthday. Sure enough, it was five thirteen in the afternoon. He'd been at it for five hours, five bloody hours, and hadn't even made a dent.

Bugger.

Exhaling a long, suddenly exhausted breath, he reclined back in his seat and pushed a hand through his hair. He supposed he should follow their lead and go home. This work could wait a night, and Alice would be on her way home soon enough, after she'd picked up Alex from her parents and battled her way up the stretch of M5 that connected Bristol and Gloucester, through the last of the rush hour traffic. They'd have a nice family dinner before sitting down to… what? Talk about their day?

That's good darling. My day? It was ok. I struggled a bit with that report, but Rebecca gave me a blowjob when she popped by. So all in all…

The thought had a dry laugh billowing up his throat.

How could he look Alice in the eyes again? Hold their son again?

No, he couldn't. Not now, not after…

The computer emitted a small double ring and an email notification window popped up in the bottom right-hand corner of the screen. It was from Scarlet, though the address attached read *Tight_Ass_Bitch*.

Officially, no one knew who had hacked her email to change the address. Whoever it was though, their joke had backfired. Far from being annoyed or embarrassed by the stunt, Scarlet practically adopted the title, and never missed an opportunity to live up to it.

True to her unofficial title, the message was brief and to the point.

Dick
Drop by my office on your way out.

We need to discuss Prometheus.
Scarlet

"... Shit," Richard cursed and looked mournfully back to the paperwork and the potential overtime it offered. "Well, that puts the kibosh on that plan."

He closed the mail with a click of his mouse.

The door was sleek pine with a bronze plaque embossed with the legend, *S. Holmes, Accounts Supervisor*.

Being the boss's daughter certainly had its perks.

Richard knocked once, then pushed on through without waiting for an answer.

Seated at the immense leather-topped oak desk that dwarfed her and the rest of the office, Scarlet was working on her laptop. Behind her, floor to ceiling windows boasted a picturesque landscape of the river below.

To a stranger, she might have looked oblivious, blind to the goings on around her, her focus dominated by her work, but Richard knew better. Scarlet was anything but oblivious. She was the sort of woman who woke up intending to conquer the world. Who missed nothing.

Without waiting for an invitation, he crossed the wood panelled floor, bypassing the plush leather sofa to take the simple leather and teak chair opposite her side of the desk.

She didn't look up, nod, or do anything to acknowledge his presence.

Nor would she. Not yet. Not until she was ready.

It was her game, a power play to remind the minion just who was the boss.

Well, at least she didn't make him pass her tea or pick pens off of the floor.

The office had been the department's briefing room before her appointment. Her predecessor had made do with the windowless coat cupboard three doors down. It was simple and functional, but large enough to impress. And beige. Very beige. Beige walls. Beige rugs. Beige leather…

Beige. Safe and soothing, and not at all Scarlet Holmes.

She was as bloody crimson as her namesake. And then a dash extra.

All heat and passion and searing raw emotion. And beauty.

Scarlet flaunted flawless skin, tanned to a soft peach hue, that complimented the waves of spun gold that tumbled down to her shoulders. She wore a tight white dress that showed off plenty of leg and had a deep plunging neckline to emphasise her figure. There wasn't a man alive who could deny Scarlet was *very* lovely.

The matter wasn't up for discussion. It was a fact.

And only skin deep.

Beneath the fragile beauty, she was as hard and sharp as steel. A lioness disguised in a little bunny's fur.

He ignored the urge to check his watch. That subtle hint would only prolong the game, though. Scarlet would see to that, sure enough. So instead, he amused himself by watching the goings on outside the tall windows behind her desk that overlooked the line of narrow boats and yachts moored along the Sharpness Canal.

The view was wasted on Scarlet.

When she turned to him, the bunny beamed up at him. "Hey Dick."

"Hi Scarlet," Richard smiled back, inwardly steeling himself. If she wanted to play her games, he'd play. "How was your day?"

It was a poor effort, but the best he could do on the fly. It got the job done.

"Oh, the usual, same shit, different day. You headin' home for the day?"

"Yeah soon, just had a couple of things I wanted to finish up first."

She ignored the prompt and just kept smiling up at him.

Sod it, she could have this round. "So, you wanted to see me?"

Her eyes were bright, and they laughed at him behind her glasses. She didn't need them. The lenses were from a cheap pair of reading glasses she'd got in a Pound shop, but the frames were designer and worth more than he made in a month. "Yes, we need to discuss Prometheus."

"Oh? How come?"

"Don't play coy with me, Dick." Despite her smile, behind the cheap plastic lenses, her eyes flared with blue fire. Behind the bunny, the lion was baring its fangs, a warning before the charge. "I told you I wanted you to make the Prometheus Account your top priority, yes?"

"Yes."

"Yes? That was a month ago. The report should have taken you a few days, max. And now you send me this?" She pulled a manilla folder out of a drawer and laid it open on the desk. A quick glance confirmed it was the paperwork he'd sent her earlier. "So, what's the game?"

"Game?"

"You could have knocked this up in a few hours. You have been, all afternoon. So, either you had a hunch, then lost your nerve, or you were slacking off to make me look bad. Which is it?" Closing the folder, she slid it aside, then leaned forward to face him, fingers tipped by perfectly manicured nails painted speckled gold, steepled under her chin.

"Scarlett I…"

"Do you have a problem working under me, Dick?"

"No."

"Then you had a hunch?"

"It was a stupid idea, not worth mentioning."

"You thought it was important enough to risk the contract."

Reaching into his pocket, he pulled out the flash drive with all his research into Prometheus and laid it on the desk. He'd forgotten about it amongst everything else that had gone on in the last couple of days and had only thought of it after receiving her email. He'd brought it along just in case. "It's nothing."

"Why don't you let me be the judge of that." She took the flash drive and plugged it into her desktop. With a few clicks of her mouse, all the documents were arranged on her monitor. Spreadsheets. Invoices. Tax returns. Everything he could find on Prometheus, but would it be enough?

A tight knot of tension wound around and around his guts like a python's coils. Financial reports. Richard watched her work. Those fierce blue eyes skimmed over the screen behind her glasses, moving from one article to the next while she caught her rose-pink lower lip between a perfect set of pearly whites.

He hated to admit it, but her look was sexy as hell.

She swivelled slowly back around in her chair to face him; her stare piercing. Not quite a lioness, but definitely not a flopsy bunny either. "All this shows is Prometheus recorded substantial profits. Hardy conclusive, *Dick*."

A low shiver coursed down his spine to tingle in his crotch as his cock stirred at the way she said his growingly official nickname. The accusation behind it made him feel like he was getting a telling off from the hot teacher all the boys fantasised about.

"Since the early 90s, Prometheus has consistently recorded growing profits. Yes, however, if you look more closely, you'll see the bulk of their earnings came from work throughout Ukraine, Estonia, Georgia, Kazakhstan, and the Baltic states. Nations recovering from the Soviet Union. Plenty of cheap labour, but a brassic economy. Prometheus's books took a slight hit in the Global recession but remained firmly in the black until 2012, when they expanded their operations into the Middle East. Work in areas of Turkey and Syria achieved record profits, despite the numerous conflicts raging in the region." He paused, trying to think how to put the next part.

"Go on…"

He took a breath, steeling his nerves for the plunge. "I think Prometheus has connections with Russian organised crime and is a front for criminal activity, including money laundering, drug trafficking and smuggling."

And there it was, the complete ruin of his career. And all packed up neatly in one sentence. Who says experience counts for nothing!

For the longest moment, Scarlet let the silence drag on. Her expression impassive, unreadable, neither bunny nor lion, but her eyes, once such a vibrant blue, were suddenly steel. "I see." Her tone was as cold and sharp as ice. "Those are very serious accusations, Dick. Ones we're required by law to report to the proper authorities and would almost certainly result in us losing the client, even if you're wrong. Can you prove this?"

"No," he confessed, then added hastily. "But there are too many anomalies for it all to be just coincidence."

"What anomalies?"

"The company was founded in the early 90s and received heavy outside funding, primarily from a now disbanded Russian-led consortium, at the same time Russian gangsters started moving west out of Moscow. They do business all over Europe but are especially affluent in areas of high Russian criminal activity and interest."

Scarlet nodded. "And their 2012 expansion?"

"The date they began expanding was just a month after the Russian President's second inauguration. It's not exactly a secret he uses the crime bosses as off the book enforcers, and the countries Prometheus has expanded to have seen heavy Russian influence since."

"They're war zones, Dick," she laughed without mirth, shaking her head. "Builders and developers often receive government contracts to repair and rebuild sites damaged in conflict."

"Yes, but usually after the war is won," Richard cut in. "I've heard of prudent planning, but if I'm wrong, whoever picked these deals must have one hell of a crystal ball. You should take him to the Cheltenham races next year. With this guy's luck, you'll make a fortune betting on the gee-gees."

She ignored the joke, instead turning back to look over the documents on her screen. "Well, the money laundering is self-explanatory. Dirty money finances the projects on the books, then returns as profits, but what about this trafficking and smuggling nonsense?"

What? Was she actually buying this story? He couldn't believe it; he'd half expected her to tear up his contract right there, even for suggesting it.

"They ship out their own equipment instead of hiring or purchasing on-site. A JCB is a pretty big bit of kit. Lots of places to hide something you don't want found, if you know how."

"But you can't prove it. Legally."

"No." His throat was so tight, he had to force the word out. "After tax is accounted for, their profits are all funnelled into an account in a private Depository Bank in Zurich. I can't track it from there without going through a long and costly legal battle."

"So…" she rounded on him, her voice as cold and sharp as steel. "Let me get this straight, because I'm a little confused. You're given a high value contract, told to make them your top priority, but instead of doing your job and having the report on my desk like you're supposed to, you dig into their business records and concoct some cock and bull theory about the Russian Mafia. And just to put the icing on the cake, you have no proof? Nothing to back it up. Is that about the sum of it?"

"More or less."

She sighed and shook her head.

That was it. She'd just fired her broadside and hit dead centre. He was sunk. He might as well go back and clear out his desk. Save the trip in tomorrow and have a lie in-

"Why did you keep digging? Why not just hand it in when you were supposed to after hitting a dead end?"

Richard had to work hard to keep his confusion from showing.

Why had he kept digging? Force of habit? Professional curiosity? His last job had done checks all the time, and he'd never let it go on for so long. There had just been something. Something not right. Something he couldn't put his finger on. Just something. Just…

"Just a hunch."

"A hunch?" She leaned back in her chair. "Well Dick, I don't know what to say, except…" Her full red lips spread into a wide smile, with just the hint of a white lion's fang. "Congratulations."

Chapter Five

Richard blinked, almost at a loss for words. Almost.

Congratulations? For what? Dropping a bollock? Making a complete ass of himself? "What?"

Scarlet's head titled, her eyes dancing and gleeful, both bunny and lioness. "Congratulations. You passed the test."

"Test? What test?" he demanded, incredulous.

"For the position of Financial Analyst," she said simply. "You applied for the position before being assigned to this department."

"Yeah, I remember."

How could he not?

It had been one of the few jobs he'd actually wanted. Similar seniority to his old role, but with a better salary and abundant career opportunities.

Or so the ad in the job centre had led him to believe.

What they'd offered was a polite brush off, followed by a role that was a major move down, with less pay, more hours and with every opportunity he could ever have hoped for, to kiss ass and get his ass kicked. However, with little

Alex on the way, what choice had he had? It wasn't like he was getting headhunted by the Bank of England, after all.

"But that was over a year ago." he added, only just able to keep the bite from his tone.

Scarlet nodded, leaning back in her chair. The bunny had taken flight now. She was all lioness here, a queen in the heart of her territory, mistress of all she surveyed, and those hot, ice-blue eyes watched him keenly over her steepled fingers. "As you are aware, the role requires certain aptitudes. Qualities that are difficult to assess on a CV and in an interview. So, potential applicants are allocated a minor role in the company, then in due course, we allocate them a manufactured account to evaluate their performance."

"Hence Prometheus," Richard nodded, comprehension blooming. "Who seduced Zeus with plates of bones wrapped in fats to give offal covered beef to humanity."

"Then stole fire, and was punished by being chained to a rock for the great eagle to feast upon his liver each morning," Scarlet added.

"Very symbolic. So, if the candidate lacks the predisposition for the role, they're fed to the eagles?"

"More or less," she purred with a subtle tilt of her head that made Richard wonder if she wasn't entirely joking. "But, congratulations Dick, you've passed the test. Though I have to say, you were taking your sweet time about it. I was about ready to chuck your ass to the curb on general principle. Rather ironic, really. If you hadn't, you certainly would have been after I read what you sent me earlier. How long did all this take you?"

"About a day and a half," he shrugged, feeling very warm in his suit. It all made so much sense and was now so obvious. God, how could he have been so stupid? Russian organised crime. He must have lost his mind.

"Extraordinary. That's half as long as the last guy who passed the test." Shifting back in her chair and crossing her legs, revealing a lot of her soft, golden thigh, Scarlet brought a hand up to toy with a lock of her hair, studying him with renewed interest. "I must say, though, yours is certainly the most unique report yet. And all from the financial data you were provided and a bit of digging. Just extraordinary. You certainly have a vivid imagination for an accountant, Dick. You've been reading too much Andy McNab. Still, I might just have to commission you to write a novel." The corner of her mouth curled in the ghost of a smile and the tip of her pink tongue swept over her plump, juicy, pink lips. "A seedy little erotic thriller. Perhaps about a businessman caught cheating on his wife."

She let the suggestion hang there, but held his gaze just long enough for Richard's blood to turn to ice in his veins.

Shit.

Was it just a coincidence? Or did Scarlet know something? No, that was crazy. How could she? He was being silly. She couldn't know anything about him and Rebecca, unless- the sound he'd heard outside the office door. Someone moving around behind the door… Had it been Scarlet? Fuck.

 "So… I'm getting promoted?"

Smooth, very smooth, asshole.

Whatever Scarlet had been expecting, that wasn't it.

She laughed.

She actually laughed. A soft, kittenish, and unmistakably feminine sound, as fair to the ears as she was lovely to behold. It was the first time Richard had ever heard it and despite his rather precarious situation; it surprised him to find the sweet melody suited her and made her appear more delicate.

He almost forgot what a bitch she could be.

Almost.

"Not quite," she chuckled. "Consider it more of a lateral move. You'll remain in my department, but within a role more suited to your talents. Get a nice little pay raise, your own private office three doors down the hall. Just what you need, a little *privacy…*"

"Is that a prerequisite for the position?" Richard asked, his throat growing tighter.

She giggled softly. "In your case, Dick, I think it's indispensable."

She was baiting him, daring him to ask the question. Both manoeuvring and mocking him. Just another game. Fuck, fuck, fuck!

"If you say so," he said simply, sidestepping her trap by the skin of his teeth. *Great, now all I've got to do is get the hell out of Dodge.*

He just needed an excuse.

Just one polite reason to-

Scarlet's lips twisted wryly. "Very good Dick, but as much as I'd like to sit here engaging in a bit of witty repartee with you, I don't have the time and you don't have the wit, so why don't we just cut through the bullshit." She removed her glasses and placed them on the desk before turning her computer monitor around for him to see.

Oh shit…

A video file was open on the screen, paused for the moment, but Richard recognised it as the feed from a security camera, a camera from his office. The camera that just so happened to be looking down at his cubicle. Where he was sitting… with Rebecca in his lap.

How could he have forgotten about the damn cameras?

Scarlet clicked her tongue, the lioness's merciless blue eyes fixed on him. "Now Dick, I don't care what my staff get up to on their lunch. Frankly, if you're off the clock, I don't give a fuck… so long as it takes place off company property."

She clicked her mouse, and the feed started replaying the scene. There was no sound. The audio was redirected to a pair of buds in the jack, but then again, he didn't need it.

Every moment was still seared in his memory. Him and Rebecca making out in his chair. The call from Alice. Rebecca hiding. His wife stripping on the screen while the girl sucked him off… Richard hated to admit it, but even under her scrutiny, the memory of it was making him hard.

"Off the record, I have to say, I'm impressed. I thought the pair of you were just a boring, straight-laced, middle-class couple. The sort that argues twice a week and fucks once every leap year. I certainly never would have guessed Alice had it in her. I mean, I always suspected she had a bit of a wild streak in her. All these stuck-up bitches do, but to actually Skype her man at work to have phone sex! Bravo. And as for you…" She shut down the media player and twisted the monitor back around to face her, her eyes bright and mocking. "Well, look at the cock on you. And while a hot bit of young ass blows you under the desk, as well. Never knew you had it in you, either. I thought that only happened in bad porn."

With a shudder of self-loathing at his treacherous loins, Richard met Scarlet's gaze. "And I never guessed you were such a voyeur. What do you do, sit around here watching us all day?"

"No, not unless I have due cause to check the feeds. And when I spotted your little friend going into one of my departments, then strutting by my office door with that 'cat that got the canary grin' on her face nearly half an hour later… Well, it wouldn't be very professional of me to just turn a blind eye. Who knew what she was getting up to, or rather, who was getting into her…" she chuckled mockingly. "You should thank me, Dick. If someone in security had seen this. Well, who knows how far it could have gone…" She let the point hang there to let his imagination do the rest.

"Is that what happened to you? Did one guard catch you having a bonk and run off to tell Daddy?" The words were out before he could stop himself.

"Excuse me?"

Shit, now he'd done it.

He gritted his teeth against another outburst and tried to look contrite. "Never mind, I-"

"No, go on, *Dick*," she said, raising a hand to stop him, her voice suddenly very still and deadly serious. "So just what are they all saying about me? I'm the office slut? A hot fuck in the closet, or a quick suck in the bog type of girl? Or is it the old chestnut, daddy issues? Sleeping with all of Daddy's little minions because old Walrus Face wouldn't buy her a pony for her tenth birthday?"

"No one said anything about a pony," he admitted, resisting the urge to look away as a chill crept up his spine and he had the unmistakable feeling of shrinking into his chair.

"Then you've missed some of the more lurid variations," she continued. "No Dick, I've never been caught on camera. I'm not a slut, *Dick*. I just like sex and I'm not afraid to show it. Or enjoy it."

Richard wondered for a moment if he should ask, but she spoke with such resolve, he couldn't help himself. "And the stories about you with Tommy Cox, and Mike from Legal."

She shrugged. "They're true. I found them attractive and thought they would be a decent lay. So, I offered, and they took me up on it. They were under no obligations."

Richard was aghast. "They lost their jobs and their wives divorced them because of your affairs. Doesn't that bother you?"

"No!" Scarlet held up a dismissive hand. "Their wives divorced them because they found out their husbands were getting some on the side and didn't like it. And I sacked them because they thought banging the boss's daughter whenever she needed to take the edge off gave them the right to talk shit about the company. Clearly, they were wrong. If their wives had sucked their dicks once in a while, maybe they would've gone home to them instead of meeting me in the Travel Lodge. So, what do I have to feel guilty about Dick? I'm not married and I'm not lying to my spouse to bang a hot bit of ass." Her smile dropped, and her expression was suddenly as cold and hard as a diamond. "It's rather hypocritical, don't you think, questioning my morals when you're the one getting a little lip service from your bit on the side?"

She had it right, of course. And whatever else his faults might have been, Richard wasn't so great a fool as to try lying to himself.

What right did he have to criticize her?

They may have both been indiscreet, but she was single and a free agent.

He, on the other hand, was a married man.

"Yes. You're right, I'm sorry, and it won't happen again," he capitulated and finally looked down at his feet, running a hand through his hair. Scarlet nodded, accepting his apologies, but it wasn't enough. He felt the need to say more, to explain himself, or perhaps just get it all out in the open. "This all started Friday night, after we got home from the party, and I let myself get carried away in the moment. I made a mistake and now- "

"Why?"

"What?" The question was so unexpected, he rounded on her without thinking.

Yet Scarlet merely looked back, nonplussed. Then, as if he hadn't spoken at all, she calmly pulled open one of her drawers and pulled out a Tupperware tub and a small packet of chocolate dip. "Do you mind? I had lunch but seem to have missed dessert, courtesy of your little show."

He nodded, but without waiting for his response, Scarlet had already stood up and was walking around the desk to sit on the edge directly in front of his chair. She crossed her legs. "So, why was it a mistake?"

"You have got to be joking," he stammered, all too aware of their closeness as the floral scent of her perfume fogged his senses.

"Am I laughing?" she asked, undoing the container's fastenings before carefully balancing the lid on her knee like a plate, then tipping a variable punnet of fat red strawberries out onto it. "If I were joking, Dick, you would be in stitches. Now, this girl-"

"Rebecca," he cut in, perhaps a little too forcefully, but he didn't care. He didn't want her referring to Rebecca in that way. Like she was insignificant.

Scarlet shot him a withering, almost pitying look as she ripped the lid off of her dip. "Okay, *Rebecca*. You've known her a while?"

Richard nodded. "Yeah, she lives in our building. She's our babysitter."

She exaggerated rolling her eyes, then plucked up one strawberry and plunged it in the dip. "I never would have guessed, still I suppose a cliché is a cliché for a reason. Okay, so you've known her a while. And she comes from a troubled home?"

"Y-you could say that," he trailed off for a second as he watched her bring the fruit up to her lips, her tongue sliding out to taste the chocolate. He forced himself to look away, his eyes quickly fixing on a point out the window. There wasn't anywhere else he could look. Her perch on the desk caused the already tiny skirt to rise higher while placing the swells of her breasts just at his eye level...

"Abuse?"

"Something like that. Her old man isn't much cop with men, but he can be a hard one with women."

"You sound like you don't like him." She bit down on the berry and moaned a low sound of pleasure that seemed to thrum down his spine, all the way to the base of his cock.

"We've had words." Actually, Richard had caught the little bastard threatening to beat his daughter black and blue after he'd had a few too many, and she'd come home late. So he had explained, from one father to another, that that wasn't any way to treat his daughter.

The guy had gotten the message, at least for a while. However, the sounds from their flat had been growing more and more volatile recently. No doubt he would have to reiterate that little lesson before long.

She popped the rest of the strawberry into her mouth, her tongue skimming out to lick up the single roll of sweetness that was creeping down her chin. "And I suppose her mum just sits there and lets him bully her around?"

"No, her mother buggered off and left her alone with the short-arse, went to live with a boyfriend in Leeds or Bradford or somewhere up North. Rebecca hasn't seen or spoken to her in years."

She pondered that for a moment, before picking up another strawberry and nibbling it thoughtfully. "No other family?"

"None," he swallowed, his mouth and throat growing dry as the office seemed to grow hotter by the second.

"Then I don't see the problem," she declared, then slowly took the whole berry into her mouth. "She seems smart enough, enough not to think you'll leave your wife for her. She's just confused, as most girls her age are. I dare say you're the strongest male role model she's ever had and can't quite work out how she feels about you. Give her a few weeks to work it out, and she'll meet some boy her own age. But if you tell her it was all a mistake, you'll probably just do more harm than good for the poor girl."

"And what about Alice?"

"Do you love her?" She forewent the fruit entirely this time and dipped her finger into the dip.

"Of course I do, but-"

"Would you leave her for this girl or try to lead either of them on?" Scarlet put her chocolate-covered finger into her mouth and sucked it clean with a long slow draw that had Richard's fists clenching in his lap.

"Never," he rasped, his gaze focusing on those pouting pink lips, and for the briefest moment, he wondered what that lush mouth would look like wrapped around his dick.

She shrugged. "Then? What about her? Sex isn't a luxury, Dick. It's a necessity. The body needs it like it needs food and water. If you're not getting any at home, then you need to look for it elsewhere. If having a little on the side gets the urge out of your system, just enjoy the adventure while it lasts."

"Spoken like a woman who's never been married."

Scarlet smirked triumphantly and gestured at him with another plump strawberry. "And who never wants to. Humans aren't monogamous by nature, so why should I be? Just because society demands it? I'm a girl with needs who doesn't like to be tied down, and matrimony is one big leash, Dick, especially when there are so many men out there I haven't tried yet."

She dunked half the berry into the dip. "Besides, what good would telling her do? Cheaters say being honest is the right thing to do, but all they really want is to make themselves feel better about fucking up. She'll be happier not knowing."

"It's still wrong."

"How so? Is it wrong to grab a bite on the way home even though your wife is cooking dinner? No. You're hungry, so you eat. Why should sex be any different?" Her eyes then sparkled with mischief as she nibbled along the chocolate. "If it bothers you so much, just grow a pair and tell her. Or try for a three-way?"

"Now I know you're joking."

"Why not? It would certainly solve all your problems," she teased, stretching out one long graceful leg, the toe of her high-heel shoe, white to match her dress, brushing along his thigh and down his leg. "And it's certainly not adultery if your wife's banging her, too."

"Except Alice would cut my balls off and wear them as earrings," he breathed, forcing himself to look into her eyes, refusing to look down, all too aware of the unobstructed view she was offering him. Sharon Stone couldn't have done it better herself.

Holding his gaze, she leant forward until they were almost nose to nose. "I don't know. From what I saw, she's definitely full of surprises. It's always the up-tight ones that you've got to watch."

"Drop it Scarlet," he warned, gritting his teeth, his dick hard and tight and impossible to ignore.

"Am I right, Dick? I am, aren't I? Yeah, I bet she turns into a little nympho the moment her hair comes down." She dropped the plate of strawberries on the desk and reached out to finger his tie.

"Scarlet… I'm warning you." His throat was tight around the words as his heart pounded in his ears. Shit, he needed to get out of here. She was too close, he couldn't think, couldn't breathe, her damn perfume was fogging his head.

Damnit, why did she have to smell so good…

"Mmm… you know you're cute when you're flustered." She closed the gap, sliding off the desk and onto his lap so the crotch of her dress pressed against his cock through his trousers. "Come on, Dick, don't be greedy. She'll love going down on your little babysitter while you fuck her like a bitch in hea-"

Her taunt died in a surprised gasp as he seized a fistful of her blonde hair.

Chapter Six

"Shut up."

"Dick!" Scarlet hissed. "W-what're you doing?"

"I said, shut your fucking mouth." His voice was low and deathly calm, a cocktail of anger and lust pulsing through him like nitro-glycerine. Richard lurched to his feet, towering over her…

Except Scarlet wasn't a woman to be dominated.

She was a fighter.

She'd fought every day of her life. Against her brothers, against peers who thought her beneath them, against subordinates and superiors alike who thought of her as an entitled and a spoiled brat. It was why she had fought so hard to graduate top of her class at Cambridge. Why she had taken this entry-level role in her father's company and would work her way to the very top, rather than just let him marry her off.

She wouldn't be cowed or humbled or let any man take advantage of her.

The moment her feet touched the ground, she pivoted, twisting free of his grip, her arm sweeping out, nails hooked to claw his face. She attacked with all the swiftness and ferocity of a cornered cat.

However, Richard was faster, twisting out of her reach, grabbing her wrist and dragging it around behind her back, forcing her down across the desk. Before she could fully comprehend what just happened, he was leaning over her, caging her there, pinned against the desk, his body deliciously hard beneath his suit.

"Scream, and I'll gag you," he warned, fettering both her wrists in one hand while the other tugged at his tie, loosening the noose.

"You wouldn't dare." Scarlett shot him an angry look over her shoulder, even as the raw emotion in his voice made her knees weak. No man, or woman for that matter, had ever been this way with her. She'd never known getting dominated could be such a turn on.

Who'd of ever guessed he had it in him?

Richard stared her down, his gaze fixed on that pretty little mouth of hers, her luscious lips just the right size and shape for sucking cock. He was sorely tempted to gag her anyway on principle alone, but he had a better idea.

He was sick of all her bullshit, her teasing, her constant shots at Alice. He might have fucked up, possibly ruined his marriage, his life, and be about to fuck up his career a whole lot more, but that didn't give her the right to belittle his wife. This time, she'd gone too far.

It was time to teach the *Tight Ass Bitch* a lesson.

"Wouldn't I?" A dark grin pulled at the corner of his mouth as he pulled the tie over his head and looped it round Scarlet's wrists in a simple slip knot. "You've been a very bad girl, Scarlet. Do you know what I do with bad girls?" He drew back to stand over her, one hand braced against the small of her back, holding her and her wrists down, the other pushing up her skirt, bearing the lush curves of her naked derriere.

"What?" she gasped, shaking, heat and embarrassment crackling through her, making it impossible for her to stay still.

"This." His hand swept down, slapping her right cheek with a loud crack. "I give them a spanking."

Scarlet couldn't help giving a little gasp. It didn't hurt, not really, but the hot sting made her clit pulse within its hood and she twisted against her bonds, trying to give the little bud some much-needed attention. "*Dick*… I'm your boss-ah!"

He smacked her ass again, the left cheek this time, and *harder*.

"No, Scarlet," he growled, trying to ignore the way her lovely derriere, now marred by a pair of red handprints, was wriggling against the bulge of his cock. Damnit, had she noticed? This would all be for nought if she knew she was affecting him too. He reinforced the assertion with another slap that actually made her jump. "You're a bad girl. Say it."

"No." Scarlet shook her head, but when the blow came, the delicious slap of skin meeting skin and the explosion of heat was too much. She bit her lip to hold the moan at bay, but there was no stopping the slickness between her thighs.

"Say it."

Slap!

"I-I…"

Slap!

"Say it!"

Slap!

"I'm a bad girl!" she moaned, the words flowing from her as thick and sweet as honeyed cream. God, why did it have to feel so good?

Richard raised his hand, then held it there. "Again."

"Mmm… I'm a bad, bad girl!" Biting her lower lip, Scarlet chanced a glance back, her eyes pleading, but for what? Mercy, or perhaps another smack.

His hand dropped to brush over her buttocks. She instinctively flinched away from his touch but relaxed when his fingers began kneading her backside, massaging away the heat. "You admit you've been bad?"

"Yes… very… mmm… bad…" Scarlet purred, pushing back against his hand as he made larger and larger circles. She was so turned on, so wet. What was he doing to her? Why was he making her so horny?

"Teasing me. Trying to seduce me. Belittling my wife." His hand slid down between her legs, fingers reaching, feeling, sliding along her wetness, pushing through her grasping heat.

"*Yes!*" Scarlet gasped, her whole world shrinking down to the feeling of his finger filling her, stroking her delicate inner tissues, swirling and stirring her into wild delirium. Greedy for more, she wriggled and circled against his swirling digit, spreading her legs wider, opening for him.

"That's it, you bad girl, and who's the boss now?"

She swallowed, her body clenching around the digit, the tension building inside her. "You are."

"Again," he growled, curling his finger to brush over that patch of rough tissue under her clit while thrumming the bundle of nerves with the pad of his thumb.

Scarlet gasped, her eyes widening as a fog settled over her thoughts. Sensation rippled outward from wherever he touched, only threatening to crash over her, driving her to the brink. Just not over it. It was the sweetest torture, the cruellest ecstasy.

No one had ever done this to her before, made her feel so vulnerable. It was delicious. "You… You're the boss… *Richard!*"

He couldn't remember the last time she'd used his Christian name. And the way she said it, so pleading and desperate, had his lips twisting in a dark grin before he leant down over her to lick the shell of her ear. "Good girl." He withdrew his finger.

Panic flaring inside her, she twisted right and left, trying to grab his hand, but the tie held strong. "No! Don't stop…!" She yelped as he swatted her arse again, the sting dissolving into delicious throbbing pleasure.

"Are you talking back to me? Bad girl," He growled, his tone low and primal, all but tearing at his belted trousers to liberate his cock. Taking himself in hand, he rubbed the crown along her slick, greedy cleft, the tip sliding through her swollen folds to graze her little bundle of nerves, making her shudder and gasp.

"No… please… Sir… mmm… don't stop… feels so good… I…" Panting, her pussy hot and throbbing, begging, no *demanding* more, Scarlet pressed back, circling her hips, desperate to feel him slid inside her, filling her, pounding her.

It did no good. He had her pinned to her desk, caged by his body, hands bound, completely at his mercy, and it only made her burn hotter.

"What? What do you want, Scarlet?"

"Please…" she heard herself beg. Her throat tightened around the word as she turned to look back over her shoulder at *him*.

This couldn't be the man she knew.

Her subordinate, dependable Richard Martin. The quiet, mild-mannered guy who never gave her a second look. That guy was fun to tease and torment, but did nothing for her, despite his thick dark hair, chiselled bone structure and broad build.

This man, who was now almost nose to nose with her, was different. Everything about him excited her. The way he looked at her, handled her, and just completely dominated her.

God, this couldn't be happening. Who was this man? What was he doing to her? She didn't do things like this, never at work, and she was never submissive in sex. She needed control. Her lovers were quiet and submissive, little more than tools for her pleasure, dildos with a pulse. They couldn't make her beg.

Yet this man had. And fuck, why did it feel so good?

"Louder," Richard pressed, enjoying the moment, relishing the turnaround, the power. He loved hearing her like this. So desperate and needy. All her poise and professionalism stripped away to leave just the raging wanton.

She licked her lips, her eyes smouldering, dark with desire. Needing to move, to take some control, she curled her hips, desperate to stroke her clit against his crest and ease the throbbing ache pulsing there. "Please!"

"Please what?" he asked, the deep growl of his tone sending hot shivers through her core as, bending his knees, he lined himself up, the broad tapered head of his cock nestling between her folds. Just one push and he would be buried inside her.

Scarlet couldn't bear it.

"Fuck me… please, fuck me-oh!" Scarlet gasped, her eyes widening and mouth falling open in a long moan as his hips snapped forward, driving in deep. The delicious shock of his cock sliding home rushed over her, making her head spin.

Too deep. Oh God, he's huge. How the hell does Alice ever ride this beast?

"Yeah, is this what you want, Scarlet?" he rasped in a low and sultry voice that just screamed sex. His hands dropped to her hips, fingers squeezing hard enough for her to feel the bite, both dragging her back and tilting her at just the right angle to take him. Not so much holding her as using her body to fuck her back onto his cock.

"Oh yes… oh yes… yes Sir!" she panted, her insides clenching, squeezing all around him, pleasure rippling out to her fingers and toes as she felt herself open to him, inch by sinfully thick, hard inch of him. Fuck, she'd never dreamed someone could fill her so completely. "Oh fuck… oh my God… yes… make me take it. I've been such a horrible boss, I need to be punished… mmm… punish that pussy with your big fucking dick!"

Richard was more than happy to oblige. "Don't worry, you're going to get everything you deserve."

Fuck, what the hell was wrong with him? He didn't dominate his lovers, didn't degrade or overpower them. This wasn't him. He'd never been like this with Alice, hadn't been like it with Rebecca… but he liked it.

"Just look at you, you bad girl. Getting fucked across your desk with your hands tied behind your back. Your snug little cunt milking my cock. You're just bloody loving this, aren't you?"

It was time to teach his boss's daughter a lesson.

She had been asking for this, well now it was time she learned to be careful what she wished for.

"Yes! Yes, I love it!" Scarlet moaned, writhing in his arms as his hips curled against her derriere. There was a momentary feeling of emptiness as he pulled back before his hands snapped her back to meet his hard thrust, making her feel every hard inch of his godly cock driving her up onto her tiptoes.

The feeling was so intense. She felt so stretched. So full.

It made her whole core pulse and tingle, and clench around him, but it was too late. He was already sliding out, almost all the way, then driving into her again, and again, until he was pounding into her greedy sex. "I'm a bad little whore… bad fucking whore… pound that pussy… it's yours-oh- oh God, yes, yes!

The orgasm came out of nowhere, rushing over her, leaving her a limp, shaking mess. He fucked her through it, drawing out her pleasure and driving her down into the desk so that her heavy breasts and stiff aching peaks dragged across the wood through her silky blouse. His body bore down on her, pinning her there so all she could do was struggle against the silk binding her wrists in a desperate need to grab something. the desk, him, anything that might give her a little leverage.

She shouldn't have liked it, but she did.

She never would have thought she could enjoy sex restrained, but this feeling of being under his control, powerless, at his mercy.

It was dark, primitive and so wild.

He knew just how to treat her.

He was splitting her open. Using her like a bitch in heat, and it was such a turn on.

She couldn't bear it. She needed to grab something, anything…

"Yeah, that's it, cum for me, you bad girl, cum all over my cock… mmm… spread that ass for me, show me your pretty little hole," Richard growled, drinking in the sight of Scarlet's bound hands grabbing her smooth alabaster cheeks, those perfectly manicured nails biting into the soft skin, spreading them wide to show him the tight rosebud nestled within.

The vision sent a hot shiver of lust down his spine, and he couldn't resist brushing it with his thumb, circling the sphincter, pushing in ever so slightly.

Scarlet could only gasp at the feeling against her pucker, the sensation causing her sex to clench around him. "Yes Sir… please, punish me, I need it… I… I…"

"As you wish."

He growled and Scarlet could have screamed as he pulled out.

Then his arms were around her and she came up and away from the desk. Then, as if she were as light as a feather, he hoisted her to her feet and walked her around the desk to the window.

"Put your hands on the glass," Richard instructed, the tie coming undone with a quick tug.

"What?" she asked, looking out the window, down across the canal, and the bustling hive of activity that was Gloucester Docks, where the whole of the city seemed to be wandering amongst bright colourful stalls.

He couldn't be serious. All it would take was just one person looking up and-

"Do it," he urged, slapping her ass again, the crack as sharp as a bullwhip and the sting enough to overwhelm caution.

She did as he commanded, bending forward slightly and pressing both hands against the window, the glass misting with her breath. "Good, now stay right where you are."

"What!" she snapped, her heart pounding in her breast. "Are you mad? The market's down there… someone might see, *Sir*."

"And I bet that gets you wet," he retorted, crouching down and nudging her thighs further apart so the musky scent of her sex fogged his thoughts. "Mmm… your cunt's all pink and slick and begging me to keep fucking her."

"No, Dick, please, that's… not fair. I don't- oh!"

He pushed a finger along her swollen folds, through her slick cream and into her lush depths, all the way to the knuckle. "Your dripping, you bad girl. Say it."

"No, please…" she panted, biting her lip to keep from moaning at the tingling shooting through her core. However, there was no resisting the choked sob as the digit twisted and curled, feeling and rubbing all of her most sensitive places at once. Nor could Scarlet stop herself from pushing back against him, her sex clenching. "Mmm… No! Wait, not here, there are so many people down there, what if someone looks up, they could see- "

"So what?" Removing his finger, he reached out and took her last few strawberries from the desk, crushing them to a juicy pulp in his hand. "Let them look, go on, let them see you for the little slut you are. Let the *whole damn city* see you for who you really are," he said, before putting his hand on her inner thigh.

"Stop… You can't… I'll scream…" Scarlet gasped, shaking as her clit pulsed at the feeling of his hand and the illicitness of the strawberry juice sliding over her skin, spreading it up her leg and over her butt. Then, it wasn't just his hands.

"Go ahead, scream all you want, that'll just make everyone look, won't it?" Richard said, following the sticky trail with his tongue, greedily licking up both the sweetness of the fruit and the salty flavour of her desire. "Maybe even someone in the office will hear and come running. Wouldn't that be something? Is that what you want, Scarlet? To prove all those dirty gossips, right?"

"No," Scarlet choked out, shaking, the throbbing of her core growing ever stronger as the slick glide of his tongue swept up her inner thigh.

"Then shut the fuck up before I gag that pretty mouth of yours," Richard barked, before pivoting and covering her swollen clit with the lush heat of his mouth.

Scarlet couldn't stand it.

His words were so dirty and crude, raw with lust. No one had ever spoken to like that.

It was such a fucking turn on.

She couldn't bear it. Just keeping her hands on the glass was torture in itself. She wanted to grab him, fist his hair, sit on his face, squeeze her tits, rub her clit, something, anything to-

"Oh… Oh my God… oh fuck-yes!" She gasped and moaned, squeezing her eyes shut against the feeling of sensory overload as he sucked hard and greedily on her little bud before lashing it with his tongue.

"You want to get caught, don't you? Yeah, I know you do. Your pussy's so juicy. Just the thought of it has your greedy little cunt all soaked. Don't pretend you don't like it. You're dripping for it…"

"No… *Dick*!... that's not- don't say things like that! Mmm… I can't help it… you're making me… oh no, no, please, if you do that… I'll…"

She was shaking, the waves of sensation crashing over her so violently her legs were in danger of giving way from under her as her fingers clawed the window for something, anything, to hold on to.

However, Richard showed no mercy.

"You'll what? Go on Scarlet, tell me," he pressed, swirling his tongue around the bundle of nerves, his hands fastening to her quivering hips, dragging them closer…

"I'll- oh fuck… oh my God… I'll… I'll…" She was mindless with the raw need to cum. And so close, when his tongue suddenly abandoned her clit to drag along her folds, the world shattered around her. "Oh God, yes, yes, fuck yes, I'm cumming, I'm cumming, I'm cumming, fuck, fuck…"

Richard tongued her through the climax, not stopping even as her hips trembled in his arms. For what he had in mind, he wanted her good and relaxed. "Yeah, that's it, go on Scarlet, cum for me, let the whole damn city see you cum!"

She bowed her head to press her forehead against the window as the waves crashed over her, the glass deliciously cold against her flushed skin. "No… please… why are you doing this to me, please, I can't take it- oh fuck, yes, yes!"

"Mmm… beg all you want, Scarlet, this is the mouth that doesn't lie." Deaf to her pleas, he buried his face in her cleft, devouring her with long deep licks, his tongue swirling while the rough of his jaw scrapped oh so deliciously along her inner thighs. "You love it. Say it."

Scarlet shook her head, but the words stuck in her throat. She was shaking, powerless against the urge to grind back onto his tongue as her clit pulsed and throbbed, pleading for just that little bit of attention to send her soaring to the starry heavens. "No! Please don't make me- oh fuck, oh fuck, okay, okay, yes, I love it, I love it! Use me, abuse me… please, please, please, I'm your naughty little fuck toy… oh God… that's your pussy, that's your pussy…"

His cock jumped at her wanton tone, but Richard pushed on regardless.

Not yet. She wasn't ready yet. Just a little more…

"So now you don't want me to stop?" he asked with a mock teasing tone, pulling back just enough to drag the flat of his tongue along her folds, from clit to base, then back again in longer and longer glides.

A shudder wracked Scarlet at the suggestion. Or perhaps it was another orgasm. "No, no, don't stop, don't stop, please, put your dick back in me, fuck me against the glass for the whole world to see, make me cum all over your big hard cock."

"No," he rasped, his tone low and primal as he worked his tongue higher, hands spreading her cheeks. "I'm not done with you yet."

"What-oh!" Scarlet gasped as warmth washed over her pucker, sending shivers racing up her spine and throwing fresh fuel on the already raging lusts. Then his tongue slid up to circle her virgin hole, teasing it with gently prods and flicks.

No one had ever done anything like this to her before. It felt strange, dirty and wrong, but so exciting. "Wait! No… no, not there, please- oh fuck!"

She panted, her back curling at the feeling of his tongue pushing through her tight ring of muscle. Then her mind went blank, consumed by the sensation of wet heat sliding in and out.

"Wow Scarlet, I've barely started rimming you and you're already drenching the floor. Who would have ever guessed you were such an anal whore, and in front of the whole city, you bad girl." He swatted her arse just hard enough for the pain to heighten the pleasure. "Just look at you, you're loving this, aren't you?"

"Yes! Yes, I'm a bad girl, your bad little slut, punish my little hole, I deserve to be punished… I deserve it… I… I-"

"Have the tastiest ass," Richard growled, leaning over her, his body caging her against the glass as powerful fingers fisted in her hair and dragged her head round. Then he took her mouth in a bruising kiss, his sinful tongue encircling hers, brushing and stroking and fogging her thoughts with his strong, heady flavour.

No, not his flavour, hers. He was forcing her to taste herself.

The revelation made her core clench at the very moment he slid inside her.

"Mmm… I could fuck your cunt all day, you bad girl," Richard groaned, his dick painfully hard and the temptation to give himself over to the feeling of his lush walls milking him was almost irresistible. Almost. Instead, he rolled his hips, stirring her grasping sheath before pulling out, his shaft slick and glistening with her cream.

Scarlet shuddered at the loss and made a pouting sound that dissolved into a low moan as he leant down to nibble the shell of her ear, hands dropping to her naked ass, spreading her cheeks for his cock to glide up, the broad crest parting her folds.

She was shaking, so on edge, her whole body was almost humming with carnal need. One little push would be all it took to push her over the edge-

"But now…" he whispered in her ear, pausing only to bite down and tug on her lobe. "I want to find out how tight your ass really is."

She stilled at the dark promise in his voice, eyes widening as the crown touched her pucker.

"Wait, you don't mean? Oh no…" she gasped, shaking her head.

"Oh yes, your ass is mine," he growled, rearing back to drink in the vision of her stretched out before him. Flushed and panting, her blonde hair had become a passionate mess and that once immaculate white business dress was rumpled the way that only a good, hard fucking could do, its skirt scrunched up around her hips to show off the full curves of her luscious, strawberry smeared butt.

It was a complete contrast from the woman he knew and filled him with a savage, primitive pride. He slid forward, pressing his slick tip against the ring of muscle. Soft and pliant from the multiple orgasms, her body opened before him.

"Oh fuck! Oh, fuck!" Scarlet gasped, her eyes going wide at the sudden burning sensation, the feeling of something hard, thick, and slick splitting her open. Instinctively, she tried to clench down, to force him back, but that only seemed to speed his invasion on, so the broad crest slid through.

"That's it Scarlet, let me in… mmm you really are a tight arsed bitch all right, but don't worry, not for much longer," Richard promised, curling his hips in small circles, trying to resist the feeling of her body wrapping around his crown, sucking him in. He needed to loosen her up first, or else this would hurt.

Scarlet could only groan. Somewhere, deep down and far away, a little voice was screaming for her to give herself over to him, to let it come, but she couldn't. She just… couldn't. He was too big. Too thick.

She'd never felt this full, so stretched. So…

She threw a look back over her shoulder at him, her blue eyes large and pleading. "S-sir, I…"

Their eyes met and she couldn't keep her gasp at bay at the wild look burning in his eyes, the warring emotions battling just beneath the surface. It was the most savage look she'd ever seen, the reflection of the beast that lurked in the heart of every man as he was visibly torn between restraint, and the instinctive desire to fuck, to rut and claim her as his bitch.

His grip on her tightened, the fingers biting into her hips, holding her still as he took a step forward, pressing her to the glass while his dick kept working back and forth, slick with their mixed juices, sending heat rushing through her.

"No, Scarlet, look straight ahead."

She obeyed, too far gone now to turn back.

Overhead, the sky had turned a deep lilac, slashed with shades of pink and orange that danced across the waters of the canal as the sun slipped away behind the horizon. Below, the fair was still in full swing and growing busier as people finished their work and came to browse amongst the stalls. Anyone could look up and see them.

Someone already was.

Her reflection stared back at her from the window, but with the face of a stranger, with flushed skin and a hooded gaze, framed by a dishevelled mess of spun gold.

Bent at the waist, she looked shameless, like a whore just begging to be fucked.

The sight was so erotic, she couldn't bear it and tried squeezing her eyes shut against the image, but it lingered, burned into her mind.

"No, watch Scarlet, I want you to see," Richard bit out, his voice low and so dark with lust that she couldn't resist. Her eyes locked to his in the glass, and his hips snapped forward, driving his cock into her heat.

"Oh!" she gasped, fighting the urge to close her eyes against the sudden rush of hot sensations. "Oh fuck… oh fuck… You're… you're in my ass… there's a dick in my… oh God, this feels so…." She could feel herself opening to take him all the way, her forbidden little hole stretching to fit him, and only him.

Richard pulled back slowly, letting half of his length slide out, then drove back in, drawing another ragged sound from Scarlet. It was a deliciously snug fit, with her inner walls wrapping around him like a fist in a warm velvet glove, squeezing him tight, trying to milk the cum right out of him with every stroke.

"Yeah… you like it, don't you?" His voice was thick and gruff, more beast than man. With each push and slide, his hands dragged her into the saddle of his hips, inch by hard throbbing inch until he was balls deep.

"Yes!" she gasped, surrendering to the sinfully wicked sensations rippling out from her ass, making her clit throb and nipples ache. "Oh my fucking God… this feeling, it's so… so intense, I- I love it…. don't stop, don't stop…"

"Don't worry, you bad girl, I won't stop…" he promised, his eyes drifting down to watch his dick sliding in and out of her forbidden little hole. "Yeah, that's it, mmm… goddamn, you're taking it up the ass like a proper little whore now."

"Oh God, yes… yes Sir, I'm your whore, please, fuck me, harder, make me feel every inch of that big cock pounding my tight little virgin ass." Not caring if they were discovered, she pushed against the window to meet each thrust, grinding herself back onto his cock.

"And whose ass is this, my little whore?"

The words came unbidden.

"It's yours, all yours. I'm your good little anal whore. Split me open on your dick, make me take it. I love your cock in all my holes!"

"All of them? Even this tight little virgin ass?" he grunted, the slap of flesh meeting flesh rising around them, his movements growing more urgent with the feeling of his release building.

She bowed her head, pressing her brow to the window, the glass deliciously cool against her flushed skin. "Yes! All of them! I love taking it up the ass for you. I'm your naughty little office whore, that just another whole for you, only you- oh fuck, oh fuck, Sir, please!"

"Please what?"

He was close, so fucking close. Not sure how much longer he could last, he pushed one hand down beneath the folds of her skirt, into the bounty of lush, wet heat. He was close, but so was she. He could feel it and rubbed her clit while fucking her with a single-minded need to make her cum just once more.

"Punish me. Sir, please punish me, I deserve it! Punish me, punish all of my holes every day." Scarlet couldn't breathe, couldn't think, she could only feel. Feel the heat and fullness moving through her ass, the waves crashing over her as rough fingers strummed her throbbing clit and turned her legs to jelly. "My ass is yours, all yours whenever you want... fuck, I'm gonna cum, oh fuck, oh fuck, I'm gonna cum on your cock, oh my fuckin... yes, yes, make me cum on your fucking cock! Fuck that ass, it's yours, all fucking yours, oh fuck, oh fuck, I'm cumming, I'm fucking cumming! I'm-oh!"

Her orgasm exploded through her, unlike any release that had come before, sending her soaring. Then she started to shake as the aftershocks claimed her, and Richard couldn't resist the feeling of her ripple around his thick, swollen cock.

"Yeah, that's it you naughty whore, cum for me, cum for me in front of the whole goddamn city- ah shit, I'm cumming too!"

He moaned, burying his cock in her one last time as he came, hard. Hard enough for small black spots to dance before his eyes.

Amidst the fog of her climax, Scarlet felt his release like a flood of heat deep inside her. It was the first time a man had ever come inside her, and she liked it.

He'd stained her, branded her with a mark that could never be erased.

It made her feel dirty, deliciously dirty.

She wanted more.

Chapter Seven

For the longest moment, Richard just watched Scarlet, the beast in him wanting to savour its victory, burning the sight of her stretched out beneath him into his memory.

Then the moment passed, and it plunged him face first into cold reality.

Oh fuck…

Scarlet looked back at him over her shoulder, her full lips half curling with that damn mocking smirk. "Mmm… was I a good little whore for you, Dick?"

"Knock it off, this… this was a mistake." He stepped back and quickly shoved himself into his trousers.

She cooed and wiggled her ass, her rosebud agape and weeping pearl tears. "*Aww…* what's the matter *Dick*, the bitch going to throw a fit if you're late?" Her eyes flashed, daring him to bite.

"Fuck you," he snapped, resisting the sudden urge to put her over his knee, his nose wrinkling as his fingers fumbled with his belt buckle.

She straightened up and turned to face him, but made no effort to straighten the skirt still hitched about her hips. "We already played that game, remember?"

She lightly teased the petals of her sex with a finger before bringing the shiny digit to her lips.

"Yeah, well, maybe I'd rather forget." He wheeled around and walked around the desk, refusing to watch, and doing his best to ignore the still obvious stiffness straining against his trouser leg.

No, he wouldn't be tempted again.

However, Scarlet would not be dismissed so easily. Coming up behind him from the desk's other side, she slid her hands around his waist to finger his shirt buttons while rising up on her tiptoes to nip his ear. "Aww… don't be like that, lover. Come on, why don't you let me take care of that for you? You don't really want to go back to Alice smelling like sex, do you? There's a private washroom and shower in Daddy's office. I could wash your back for you and-"

"Forget it Scarlet!" Richard snapped. Angry and tired of her games, he brushed her hands away and rounded on her, so they were almost nose to nose. "This never happened, got it."

Scarlet held her ground, however, her playfulness gone, melted away to reveal an expression as cool and hard as ice. All except her eyes. They burned hot and fierce. "Don't kid yourself, Dick, that was the fuck of the century, and you know it. How long has it been since Alice fucked you like that? You think your little shop girl can?" Her smile spread wide, as cruel and sharp as a knife. "You're going to want it again."

She was right. About everything.

He wanted her. How could he not? He was only a man of flesh and blood, while she was the boss's daughter.

A young woman with a future as bright as her past was murky, a beautiful girl who played men the way a croupier dealt cards.

She was intelligent, sexy, and a damn great fuck.

She was Scarlet Holmes, his rock bottom, and he'd hit it hard, in more ways than one.

Now it was time to pick himself back up again.

So he turned his back on her and walked to the office door. Pulling it open, he didn't bother to look back. "Goodnight Scarlet."

At his back, still where she had stood, he could practically hear Scarlet seething when she hissed at his back. "I always get what I want, *Dick*."

It was the first time he had ever heard her composure crack.

He knew he should keep walking, to just let it slide, but sometimes he just couldn't help himself. "Then why don't you go up to your dad's office and fuck him instead?"

"Suck my clit you son of a- "

He pulled the door shut on her rebuff, and something smacked against the door. Something heavy.

Well, there goes my lateral move…

When he arrived home, the flat was dark and quiet.

It was only a short walk from the Docks, but he'd taken a detour to the 24-hour gym in the Gloucester Quay's, for a quick shower. Free membership was one perk of working for

Holmes & Raine, and Scarlet had been right. He certainly didn't want to go home reeking of sex.

Freshly washed but still none the wiser as to what he was about to say or do, he'd practically dragged his feet all the way home. By the time he arrived at the tower block, the sun had long since gone down. Alice's car was in its usual parking spot, but a quick glance at the dark living room confirmed there was no sign of her inside. Nor Alexander.

He checked his phone to see if she'd tried to message him, but the screen stayed blank. The battery had died.

"Shit," he cursed quietly, the discovery winding his guts into a tighter string of knots. He'd been so out of it recently; he couldn't even remember when he'd last charged the phone. God only knew when the thing had died on him.

Had something happened to her? What if she or little Alex had had to be rushed to hospital? What if...

What if something hadn't happened...

What if she'd got worried because he was so late and tried to call him? What if, when he hadn't answered, she'd decided to check on him?

Just the prospect sent a cold shiver down his spine.

Had she seen them in the window? He'd been half expecting to get his collar felt the moment he'd left the building. Anyone could have seen and reported them to the police. Or perhaps he just missed her when he left the building and she'd run into Scarlet.

He had to know. He needed to speak to her. Maybe there was still time to – *what the fuck!*

He flipped on the living room light, about to plug the phone into the charging outlet there, when he heard it. A moan. Low and husky and *very* familiar.

Then the sound of wood creaking.

Bed springs squeaking

Someone calling.

Calling her name.

Then he was running through the room and down the hall to *their* bedroom door. A hard kick sent it swinging inward, and he stopped dead, his eyes widening at the sight of the bodies tangled together on the bed.

Alice… and Rebecca!

Coming soon… The Final Temptation

L.M. MOUNTFORD

OTHER TITLES RELEASED BY

THE LORD OF LUST PUBLICATIONS

John Greystoke was the DeCampo Famiglia's most feared enforcer. Then he was betrayed by those he trusted most and left for dead.

Five years later, John has escaped and started anew in Washington state.

However, his enemies are closer than he knows, and they have not forgotten about the man they called Tarzan.

However, every Tarzan needs his Jane. John might just have found his, but there is no place in her life for a man like him.

To keep her, he'll have to turn his back on that world for good, but with the demons of his past getting closer, can he become the man she deserves and still save her from his past, or will the Bratva finally take his head for their Pakhan's wall…

Age is just a number, and this collection of sinfully steamy age-gap romances will prove it...

The Lord of lust has done it again and in this anything but sweet, four book Box Set, full of forbidden Silver Foxes and sassy Cougars, he proves that age is no boundary to love, or lust.

A collection of hot and orgasmic stories by The Lord of Lust

Do you love hard men, strong women, sizzling chemistry and erotic scenes that make Fifty Shades of Grey look like five shades of beige?
Well, here you go...
7 Books, 7 hard and rugged men, 7 sizzling page turners that will have you devouring every word from start to finish...

A Tropical Cocktail Boxset

Romance is in the air in this two book Holiday Romance boxset that is all about sun, sea and sex…
Tequila Sunset
Beneath The Sheets

The battle of the Species is about to rage, and only the true alpha will come out on top in the Lord of Lust hottest new duo boxset that sees vampires and werewolves lock tooth and claw…

To all the rest of the world, Elizabeth Clarke has it all.

A successful husband. A beautiful home. And now a son off to university. She is a perfect housewife with the perfect life.

It's a lie.

Her husband is a lying, drinking philanderer who hates her as much as she loathes him. Her home is beautiful, but empty, nothing more than a gilded cage to keep her trapped in a world she never wanted.

That is, until he came back into town.

Hugh Becket.

Her son's best friend. He's hot, young, and so forbidden.

Elizabeth knows she should stay away, but when the devil comes knocking on her door in the middle of the night, what's a poor neglected trophy wife to do?

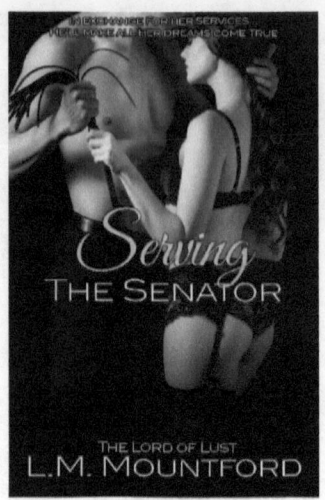

He is my Hades

I'd played the role of a goddess, bound and chained for the service of mortals.

He freed me.

He freed me, unchained me and taken me to his underworld, his dark realm where he'd brought out all my forbidden and secret desires.

And now I'm his.

His attendant. His servant…

THEIR SILENCE COMES AT A PRICE...

UNCOVERED

THE LORD OF LUST

L.M. MOUNTFORD

When Mina returns for her stepbrother's 21st birthday, she thinks her days of lusting after him are over. Caught up in the heat and passion of the moment, she is stunned to find them back in bed together; their feelings clearly far from resolved.

Haunted by her desire, Mina now has another problem… she must head down a path of lust and desire; torn between the dark delights of the handsome bad boy down the street and her adorable stepbrother who has always been there for her.

Can she confront the truth she has long tried to bury? How far will she go to save the one she wants, but knows she can never truly have?

Reckless

THE LORD OF LUST

L.M. MOUNTFORD

As an underworld princess, daughter to the boss of mob bosses all along the east coast, Sophie's life was a gilded cage. A prison of gold and silk…

That is until Luke stepped into her life.

A scrapper from the back streets, who had risen from among the ranks to stand in her shadow.

Luke, her bodyguard, and her secret lover.

Their destinies were never meant to cross, but they had. It was impossible, forbidden, but they couldn't resist…

Now their one reckless night has become a desperate fight for their lives.

THE LORD OF LUST
L.M. MOUNTFORD

I know it's wrong to want my best friend's dad… but what about when his wife offers to share?

Tracey has known the Burtons practically all her life.

They're her best friend's parents.

When she was a little girl they took her on days out to the beach. But she's a woman now, and they have some very important lessons to teach her…

'I'm sorry Cassy, but you're just too boring for me,'
That was the story of Cassandra's life.
She was always that girl. The curvy plain jane. She was fine with it,
right up until her hot bad boy ex threw it in her face before walking out
of her life. Leaving her depressed and reeling, doubting everything
about herself and her future…
So her best friend has spirited her away to her family's Gibraltar Vila
for a little fun in the sun, some much needed girl time, and a whole lot
of boys.
There's just one problem.
David, her best friend's recently divorced dad also happens to be
staying at the villa. And he's no boy…

Sooner or later, the thirst always wins…

After a thousand years, Lucian had given up any interest in the world. His only concern that night was finding his next drink, preferably from a flavoursome twenty-something with loose morals and no expectations. Then he saw her…

Kate is just a girl from the country, who came to the city with her brother to find a life away from their parents' car crash. That is, until the police came knocking on her door one morning and ripped her new life apart.

Now she has nothing and no one, with only one on her mind…

When these worlds collide, and the things that go bump in the night come calling, can these two mend the rifts in each other and give them what they need?

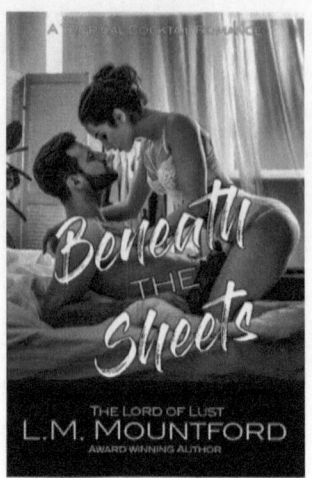

Alex's life was circling the drain, and he was officially one step away
from hitting rock bottom after finding his long-term girlfriend in bed
with his biggest clients.

Then one morning an email arrives from the last person on earth he
ever expected to hear from again.

Sarah Snow. His childhood friend, and the uncontested love of his life
whom he hasn't seen since prom night.

And before he could say travel agent, he was boarding the first plane
bound for Sydney, Australia, with nothing but his passport and an
overnight bag.

He's no idea what he'll do or say when he finally reunites with the girl
that broke his heart, but one thing's for sure…

He's not going home without her.